WHERE'S MACEEN?

A HOWARD PIERCE INVESTIGATES STORY

EVELYN INFANTE

Printed in the United States of America

ISBN #978-1-950625-37-6

Cover Design by Wesley Goulart

Publisher:

Shaggy Dog Productions, LLC
www.Shaggy-Dog-Books.com

DEDICATION

There's something oddly satisfying about pouring your heart and soul into a manuscript for weeks, months, or even years. You might toss and turn at night worrying about your characters' antics, but you know that inspiration will strike at any moment. It could come in the form of a new scene idea or a forgotten dialogue. Sometimes, it even happens in your dreams! And just when you think you've got the story figured out, you go back and read it again, only to realize that you need to rearrange the chapters or that you repeated something you already wrote. You might think, That's genius or, that sounds stupid.

Writing a book is a tough gig, that can be physically taxing, with aching necks and backs from sitting at the computer. But then, you get your hands on a copy of your published book, and all that hard work is forgotten. It's an incredible feeling to reach the finish line and see your story come to life.

In my case, putting together a story can feel like forever, but there's something that keeps me going when I want to throw in the towel. Maybe it's because I've got a bunch of writers in my family, both living and dead, who've inspired me to keep going. It's like a family tradition, you know? Or maybe it's because I simply love to write. I blame my DNA!

And you know what? the more I write, the better I get at it, and I'm always amazed at how much I can achieve if I just keep going.

So, to all you awesome writers out there who spend countless hours pouring your heart and soul into this challenging and sometimes tough writing journey, this one's for you!

Hope is the thing with feathers that perches in the soul and sings the tune without the words, and says the simple thing that must be so.

—*Emily Dickinson*

PROLOGUE

Saturday, October 24, 2009

*M*aceen Robinson tossed and turned throughout the night, her nerves preventing her from getting a restful sleep. By five a.m., she resisted the urge to get out of bed and instead forced herself to wait another thirty minutes, willing her digital clock to advance to the next minute.

At precisely 5:30 a.m., Maceen sprang out of bed and rushed to the bathroom. She splashed cold water on her face hoping to wash away any traces of a restless night, and quickly brushed her teeth. As she gently ran a comb through her long, auburn curls, she felt a sense of relief that her shower last night had spared her precious time. Dressed in the black turtleneck and blue jeans draped over her desk chair to avoid wasting time this morning, she slipped her bobby-socks-clad feet into hiking boots. However, she soon realized she had threaded them unevenly through the grommets.

"Calm down," she whispered.

Slowly inhaling and exhaling, Maceen pulled out the laces

and tried again. Boots properly laced, she checked her wrist-watch. *Better hurry.*

On this Saturday morning, her father will not rush to the depot to catch a bus into New York City where he worked the trading desk at a Wall Street Italian bank.

During the week, her mother rises promptly at six a.m. to prepare breakfast for herself and Maceen. She bids farewell to her husband, who will pick up breakfast in the city. This gives her ample time to make it to her kindergarten class. Today, however, she will keep to her weekend schedule and sleep in until seven.

Maceen made her bed, grabbed her cell phone and the prewritten note from the nightstand, and switched off the light. She then quietly closed the door behind her.

A glance at her parent's bedroom door momentarily stopped her, but she quickly recovered and tiptoed down the uncovered wooden stairs, dimly lit by the hallway's nightlight—her heart pounding in her chest with every creak of her footfalls.

Making her way to the kitchen without incident, she placed the note on the counter. Without a moment's hesitation, she swiftly walked to the hallway, turned on the light in the foyer, and retrieved her coat from the closet. She then pulled her arms through the sleeves, stuffed her cell phone into the coat's pocket, and reached for her keys hanging on the hook next to the front door.

Hands trembling, she turned off the light and locked the front door. The wind tousled her hair across her face. She wiped it away with a practiced flick and pulled up the hood of her jacket as her eyes adjusted to the dark skies. Sunrise won't occur until 7:41 a.m. If she hadn't sneaked into the garage last night to turn off the circuit breaker to the floodlights, her family, who sleep above the garage, would have been alerted to her early departure. She'd thought of everything, but life, as it often does, had other plans.

Maceen hurried to her old, well-maintained Jeep sitting on the driveway, a gift from her father when she got her driver's license. The memory of her dad's proud face when he handed her the keys and declared, "This old gal will serve you well until you get used to driving," tugged at her heartstrings, evoking a sense of sadness.

She had been hoping for a new car and had to suppress a frown as she accepted the keys from her father's hand. "I love this old car, Dad," she had feigned. Despite her initial disappointment, after a few weeks, she got used to handling the vehicle and eventually developed a fondness for it.

The Wrangler's engine noise upon startup instinctively drew Maceen's attention to her parents' bedroom windows. Despite her parents' assurances that they slept soundly even during thunderstorms, listening to the nature sounds from their Dream Machine, Maceen couldn't shake the feeling of unease.

After a moment, she slowly pulled out of the driveway, keeping her headlights off until she had left the neighborhood, unaware that eyes peeking through someone's blinds had witnessed her departure.

Maceen, who often left the house on her hiking excursions early in the morning, never ventured out before breakfast, and certainly never before sunrise. To suppress her guilty feelings, she convinced herself that her family wouldn't be worried once they read her note.

Experiencing a sense of restlessness, she took Route 611 on this tranquil weekend morning, making the trip to the Delaware Water Gap earlier than anticipated.

At the Martz Bus parking lot, she spotted his car idling a few feet from the other vehicles whose owners spent the night in New York City or had caught an early bus out of town. Her heart beat with excitement. Not in the habit of deceiving her parents, the temptation to turn around and go home was strong. However, her thirst for adventure overpowered her nerves.

She parked the Wrangler alongside his flame-red Dodge Ram and turned off the engine, forcing all thoughts of turning back out of her mind.

Climbing into the truck, he greeted her with a broad smile, a cup of coffee in one hand, and a wrapped bagel in the other.

"For me?" Maceen asked, smiling.

"I figured you might not have had the time for breakfast."

"Thank you," she said, grateful for his thoughtfulness.

He offered her the coffee container. "I didn't think you'd like it black, so I added cream and sugar. Hope I got it right."

"Yes, perfect."

"Careful, it's hot."

Maceen opened the lid and blew on the surface before taking a cautious sip. "Mmm, I needed that."

"Let me hold the coffee so you can unwrap the bagel. I made another assumption and got you a cinnamon raisin with cream cheese."

"My favorite. How did you know?"

He shrugged. "Lucky guess." He took the coffee from her hand and gave her the bagel.

"Aren't you having anything?" she asked, undoing the wrapper and folding it halfway so as not to get cream cheese on her fingers.

"I've already had mine." He tilted his head toward the backseat where he had tossed the crumbled Dunkin' Donuts bag.

Maceen shifted her body toward the backseat for a look. "I see, and I thought *I* was early. You must've gotten here in the middle of the night." She chuckled, and took a big bite of the bagel, wiping cream cheese off her lip with her tongue.

"Nah. I'm a fast eater, that's all." He offered her the coffee and turned on the radio, fidgeting with the dial.

Joe Snedeker, the meteorologist's voice announced, "Forty-two degrees on this chilly and breezy morning with winds gusting to twenty miles per hour in the backyard. Temperature today will reach fifty-five degrees with winds dying down to nine miles per hour."

"With the winds diminishing, it'll feel warmer than fifty-five," he assured her, turning the knob on the radio.

Maceen nodded, mouth full, and thought, *Fifty-five is still chilly. Glad I decided to wear my warm jacket.*

He settled on a station and cranked up the volume to the Black Eyed Peas' "I Gotta Feeling."

She bobbed her head to the rhythm as he rapped his fingers on the dashboard in perfect time to the beat.

"Love that song," she said, taking the last bite of her bagel.

"Me too."

Pulling a couple of napkins from the glove compartment and offering them to her, he asked, "Ready for an adventure?"

Trying to shake off the guilt of her secret getaway, she said, "Sure, let's go!" She finished her coffee and wiped her mouth.

Reaching back, he grabbed the paper bag and held it open. "You can put the trash in here."

After Maceen shoved the empty coffee container, wrapper, and napkins in the bag, he crumbled it closed and tossed it on the back seat.

Shifting the truck into gear, he drove out of the parking lot, just as a bus entered the lot from the other side.

1

Monday, March 15, 2010

*H*oward Pierce had been tailing Mr. Gerald Watkins for weeks, hoping to catch him without his neck brace.

Based on his social media posts filled with photos of him working out, Pierce believed Watkins would be eager to hit the gym not long after his injury claim.

Watkins drove one hour from his residence at the Delaware Water Gap to a fitness center in Allentown. Pierce snapped a few pictures with his Nikon camera as Watkins removed his neck brace, left it in his car, and headed into the gym.

"Gotcha!"

An hour later, Watkins emerged, looked around, and promptly got into his car. He secured the neck brace and departed, while Pierce discreetly activated his camera to capture the scene.

Pierce needed to catch Watkins working out to prove insurance fraud, as the photos alone would not be conclusive enough.

He needed solid evidence that would dispel any excuse Watkins could give for visiting the gym, such as his possible assertion that he was there to observe and that he was not wearing his neck brace to avoid questions about his injuries.

Putting the camera into its protective case and locking it in the trunk, Pierce pressed the car's key fob close and entered the fitness center.

A young woman at the counter, wearing a t-shirt with the gym's logo emblazoned across her chest and a tag that read, 'Dawn' pinned above her breast, flashed her perfectly straight and white-toothed smile. "May I help you?" she asked.

Pierce approached the counter. "Would it be possible to try out the facilities before making up my mind about joining?" He glanced at her name tag, "Dawn?"

Without losing her smile, she said, "Yes. As it happens, we're currently offering a one-week free promotion until the end of the month." She picked up a card and a pen from the desk. "Just print your name and sign below, and you're all set."

Pierce grabbed the items and printed his often-used alias, Howard Martel, and signed.

Dawn took the card from him and date stamped it. "You can start to work out right away."

"I'd love to, but I don't have any workout clothes with me. I'll be back tomorrow. Thank you, Dawn."

She bit her bottom lip, worried she messed up on her first week signing new customers. "I'm sorry. I thought you wanted to check us out today or I would've stamped the card with tomorrow's start date."

"Don't worry about it. I'm sure it won't take a whole week for me to decide."

Relieved, she said, "All right, see you tomorrow then. When you come in, one of our trainers roaming the floor will help familiarize you with the equipment."

"Great, thanks again."

Pierce turned as if to leave, but hesitated. "Dawn, my friend, Jerry, or rather, Gerald Watkins, recently became a member. We go way back. In college, we regularly exercised together before he moved away. I'm sure he'll be delighted to see me." He flashed her his most endearing smile. "Do you happen to know what time he would be coming in tomorrow?"

Dawn again bit her bottom lip.

Pierce mentally crossed his fingers.

"Members are free to visit the gym at their convenience, regardless of the day or time. As your friend is a new member, his schedules have not yet been recorded in our computer system."

Pierce frowned. "I understand. Never mind, Dawn," he said, taking a step back and ready to leave.

"Wait. Give me a moment."

Pierce halted.

Dawn scanned the computer for a few seconds. "Here it is. Mr. Gerald Watkins, right?"

"Yes," that's my old friend, Jerry."

"You're in luck. He reserved a spot in our weights area for tomorrow morning at 6:30."

Pierce's insides contracted at the thought of getting up before sunrise. "Reserved?"

"Oh yes. You won't believe how crowded the weights area gets before people head out to work."

"Makes sense. Thank you again, Dawn." *Jerry is in for a surprise.*

Dawn glanced at Pierce's membership card. "Goodbye, Mr. Martal," she said cheerfully. "See you tomorrow."

2

Tuesday, March 16, 2010

*A*s the morning rush hour began, people left for work, their car headlights blinding as they drove by Pierce. He had been sitting in his car parked across from the Gerald Watkins' home for twenty minutes, trying not to doze off.

At precisely, 5:15 a.m., dressed in his sneakers and sweats, and wearing his neck brace, Watkins left his residence.

Following, Pierce hung back, aware of the intended destination but keeping his target in his sights. When he arrived at the gym's parking lot, Pierce positioned his car two rows away, enabling him to witness Watkin's entry into the fitness center, sans the neck brace.

After a few minutes, Pierce, dressed in his sweatshirt and pants, and carrying his water bottle, wandered in. At the counter, he presented his temporary membership card to Mark, a physically imposing young man who displayed a remarkably radiant smile akin to Dawn's.

Perfect teeth must be a requirement to work here.

Mark stamped the card and returned it to Pierce. Without dropping the smile, he said, "Enjoy your workout."

"Thanks, Mark," Pierce said, putting the card into his pocket. "Looking forward to it."

He grabbed one of the rolled-up towels from the counter and sauntered into the fitness room, which seemed too small to accommodate the many people working out so early in the morning.

Surveying the room, Pierce noticed everyone seemed fit and trim, with hard bodies and bulging muscles in their shorts and sweats. *No newbies here,* he thought.

The ventilation system did an adequate job masking the odor of hot bodies, but the presence of a man dripping with sweat as he peddled for dear life on the stationary bike was difficult to ignore. It reminded Pierce why he preferred working out at home. But he had a job to do and redirected his attention to the weightlifting area where Watkins was training. As Dawn had mentioned, the area was indeed crowded. As soon as a person was done with their session, another person assumed their place at the benches or in front of the wall-to-wall mirrors where a couple was jumping rope. Pierce proceeded towards the treadmill area and waited for a machine that provided a direct view of the weightlifting area, where he could keep an eye on his target.

A trainer noticed him and took it as an invitation to approach. "Hi," she said. "Trying to decide where to start?"

There's that smile again.

Pierce also smiled and glanced at her name tag. "Just looking around, Sherry. First time here."

"If you'd like, I can evaluate you and draw up a specific fitness routine for your needs."

"Thank you, but I think I'll get on the treadmill today. I'm short on time."

"All right. Enjoy the treadmill," she said, walking away and looking for someone else to help.

When a woman slowed down the treadmill machine directly in line with Watkin's bench, Pierce stepped closer and nodded, indicating he was waiting. When she finished, she said, "All yours."

"Thank you," Pierce replied, and hopped on. Although he regularly did a vigorous run on his home treadmill, he kept the speed low, getting into a walking rhythm. Never taking his eyes off his target, he reached into the pocket of his sweatpants and took out his brand-new iPhone 3GS. Putting in the earbuds, he turned his head right and left, making sure no one on the nearby treadmills paid attention to him. No one did. They were busy watching the overhead televisions, reading, or listening to music through headsets, intent on their workouts.

Using his phone's video recorder, Pierce pointed it toward the weights area and, maintaining a steady hand, recorded Watkins' workout. He was amazed as Watkins effortlessly completed three repetitions of each exercise: the dumbbell bench press, bent-over row, military press, lateral raise, and pullovers. These exercises targeted the muscles Watkins claimed caused him pain from an alleged fall he suffered at a restaurant.

Pierce wondered how much longer his workout would take. Suddenly, Watkins took a swig of his water bottle and got off the bench. After wiping it down, Pierce thought the workout was complete. However, Watkins proceeded toward the treadmill area, where all the machines were occupied.

Pierce stopped videotaping, turned on the voice recorder, and shoved the phone into his shirt pocket. When Watkins approached looking for an unoccupied machine, Pierce got off the treadmill. He grabbed the nearby spray bottle and towel and began wiping down the machine.

Watkins walked over and nodded.

Holding the spray bottle and towel, Pierce stopped wiping and faced him to get a clear voice recording.

"That routine on the bench looked intense."

"Nah, just a warmup. After my weightlifting session, I usually mix things up to get my cardio in."

"Running will do that," said Pierce, with certainty.

Watkins chuckled, "Not only do I run and lift weights, but I jump rope, kickbox, and once in a while I participate in an aerobics class. I do it all. By incorporating these exercises into my routine, I can eat and drink anything I like without worrying about my weight." He proudly patted his well-defined abdomen.

"Well, you certainly look fit."

"Thanks," he said, impatient to get on the treadmill.

"Are the weightlifting exercises you were doing painful?" asked Pierce.

Watkins tensed.

Pierce promptly clarified, "I have an arthritic shoulder, so I can't lift anything heavy. I was wondering if doing some exercises like you were doing would help strengthen my shoulder muscles."

"I don't know about that. Better ask one of the trainers," he said, relaxing, "but I think you'll be fine if you take it slow 'till your muscles adjust."

"I will. Thanks." Pierce extended his hand toward the treadmill. "Enjoy!"

From his car, Pierce watched as Watkins left the gym and again put on his neck brace before driving away.

People never learn. The case is not yet settled, but he had to go to the gym.

3

Thursday, March 18, 2010

A few days after her disappearance, Maceen Robinson's whereabouts hit the front pages of area newspapers. The story captivated the community for several weeks. Her parents were interviewed on the local television station, expressing their anguish and pleading for the return of their seventeen-year-old daughter, who was widely suspected of being abducted. However, to date, neither the police nor the parents had received a ransom note, phone call, or correspondence indicating that the girl was being held against her will.

Weeks became months, and the public's attention turned toward other news. Flyers that had been posted everywhere by concerned citizens were either torn, withered, or covered over with ads promising low-interest loans, home builder ads, or pleas for information regarding lost pets.

Although the disappearance had an occasional mention on local radio, television, and newspapers, in an effort to appease the parents who were relentless in their demands to keep the story alive, without new information, the story eventually faded.

With the investigation stalled, Daniel Robinson, Maceen's father, sought advice from his neighbor, Chino Martinez. Chino suggested that the Robinsons hire a private investigator. He believed that a private investigator might be more effective in finding Maceen, as they would be working directly for the family and would be paid a fee for their efforts.

Searching the Monroe County telephone directory, Daniel shut the book and leaned back in his chair. Frowning, he closed his eyes and rubbed his forehead, trying to decide which firm to contact. A sudden memory struck him, and his eyes flew open. It was about a homicide detective who had started a private investigations firm a few years back, after retiring from the police department. Running his finger down the private investigators listings, Daniel stopped at Bloodhound Investigations.

That's it. Bloodhound.

He picked up the phone and dialed. After securing an appointment, Daniel felt confident he made the right decision. Perhaps a private investigator would look for his daughter more vigorously than the police, he surmised. However, he worried how he would tell his wife, Sakura, he had an appointment with a former homicide detective, without saying what they both feared—that their daughter had been abducted and possibly murdered.

The next day, Daniel Robinson knocked on the door of the Bloodhound Investigations' office twenty minutes before his appointment. When he entered the anteroom, Ruby, the office administrative assistant, greeted him with a warm smile. "Mr. Pierce is with a client." She gestured toward a chair. "Please, take a seat. He won't be long now."

"Thank you. I know I'm early."

"May I offer you a cup of coffee while you wait?" asked Ruby.

"No, thank you."

"Very well." Ruby pressed the intercom button to alert Pierce of Mr. Robinson's arrival, and turned to her computer, her fingers rapidly tapping on the keyboard.

Daniel nervously sat with his hands clasped on his lap, trying not to stare at Ruby's pink-colored pixie haircut or dark pink lipstick. Instead, his eyes wandered around the room, noticing but not focusing, on the coffee station across from him, the coat tree, or the plants on the windowsill. Trying to calm his anxiety, Daniel focused on the colorful lithographs on the wall, where Pierce's wife, Louise, purposely hung them believing the colors would soothe nervous clients.

Five minutes later, the door to Pierce's office swung open and a woman in her late forties, dressed to the nines in her open-jacket Halston dress, side bangs on her carefully coifed head, and diamonds twinkling from her earlobes, walked out. Pierce followed closely behind.

Walking the client to the front door, Pierce noticed the bags under Robinson's eyes and how he mindlessly twirled his wedding ring around his finger.

"Thank you again, Mr. Pierce," said the stylishly dressed client, her meticulously applied red lipstick accentuating her words.

"You're welcome," he said, holding the door open. "I'll be in touch as soon as I have some information for you."

She nodded and left.

Pierce closed the door and turned to Mr. Robinson with his hand outstretched for a handshake. "Nice to meet you, Mr. Robinson. Sorry to have kept you waiting."

Robinson stood, cleared his throat, and shook Pierce's hand. "Nice to meet you too. I was early," he mumbled.

"Come, let's chat in my office."

Once seated, Pierce expressed his sympathy for Mr. Robinson's hunger for news of his daughter's whereabouts. As a father of two girls, Pierce understood his anguish.

"I know you've spoken to the police, but please bear with me if I ask you the same questions."

"I understand," Robinson replied, with a lump in his throat.

Daniel Robinson felt exhausted from answering Pearce's questions and reliving the terrible day when he and his wife discovered their only daughter had vanished without a trace. He found solace in hiring Howard Pierce, certain that if anyone could unravel the mystery of his daughter's disappearance, it would be a former homicide detective, for better or for worse.

4

*a*fter escorting Mr. Robinson to the door and reassuring him he would do everything possible to find out what happened to his daughter, Pierce returned to his office debating whether to ask one of his former colleagues how far they had gotten with the Maceen Robinson case. With knowledge of the investigation, Pierce wouldn't need to start from scratch with what he learned from the internet and his interview with Mr. Robinson.

As he thought about it, his former second-in-command, Sergeant Ignacio Ramirez, affectionately known as "Iggy," came to mind. He was sure that Iggy would have given him the information without a second thought. However, Sergeant Ramirez had moved on from his job as the head of the homicide investigations squad, and had taken a job in Philadelphia.

Uncertain about the new sergeant's willingness to share information about an ongoing case, especially to a former detective he did not know, Pierce decided to contact one of his former team members.

He dialed the Stroud Area Regional Police Department's main number and asked for Sergeant Junjie Leung.

"The detective is out at the moment. Would you like to be transferred to someone else?" asked the operator.

Pierce considered Celia Byrne, recognizing her potential to provide him with what he needed. However, he'd wait to speak to Leung, wondering if Celia would take the chance of leaking information to her old boss. Ceci had always been a straight shooter, and Pierce was hesitant to ask her to do something she wouldn't ordinarily do. On the other hand, he might be able to persuade Leung to share information with him.

"No, thank you," he responded. "Please transfer me to his voicemail."

After three rings, a recorded message came on: "Detective Leung, SARP. Please leave your name, number, and a brief message and I'll get back to you."

"Jun, this is Howard. Please give me a call at my office when you get a chance. I need a favor. You know my number."

Pierce, eagerly awaiting the return phone call, reached for the legal pad to review the notes he had jotted down during his meeting with Mr. Robinson.

The police did not suspect foul play after a search in and around Maceen's home that would have triggered an FBI investigation. The note left by the girl on the morning of her disappearance did not specify her destination, except that she was going on a hike. Although her parents were concerned she left before breakfast and had never done so before, they assumed she wanted to get in as much hiking time as possible. According to Mr. Robinson, his daughter was preparing to hike the Appalachian Trail after graduation.

Pierce found it odd that her note did not mention her hiking group, specify the trail she would take, or explain the early morning departure.

With his years of investigative experience, Pierce's initial reaction was to suspect that the missing girl was either dead or didn't want to be found.

Although he had kept up with the news like everyone else when the girl went missing, Pierce reached for the computer mouse and searched online newspapers. An hour later, after taking down a few notes, Pearce leaned back in his chair and wondered if the police had kept any information from the public. He hoped his former colleague, Detective Junjie Leung, could provide him with more details.

There was other work Pierce could be doing but rather than shift gears, he paced, anxiously waiting on Jun's phone call. *Come on, buddy. Call me.*

The phone finally rang. Pearce grabbed it before the second ring. "Howard Pearce," he said, pulling out his chair and dropping into it.

"Sarge, it's Jun. What's up?"

Pearce smiled. Despite the years away from the job, Detective Leung still called him "Sarge."

"Jun, thanks for returning my call."

"Sure. Just got back to the precinct. Busy morning."

"Anything to do with the Robinson disappearance?"

"Robinson? Oh, no, that case's gone cold. Why do you ask?"

"Her father has hired me to look into it."

"And you want to ask me about the case," he said, his voice dry.

Pierce picked up on the sarcasm in his tone. *Better tread lightly.*

"I'm sure you guys are on top of it, but if you can share anything with me, anything at all, it would save me a lot of legwork."

A moment of silence passed. Pierce held his breath, hoping he hadn't overstepped his bounds.

Leung blew out a tired breath. "What do you need?"

"How 'bout I buy you lunch, and we can talk about it?" Pierce suggested.

"When, today?" asked Jun, in a shrill voice.

"If you're up for it."

"Hold on a minute." The phone went dead. Pearce could hear papers rustling.

Jun's voice came back on. "Yeah, I think I can make lunch. Is one-thirty good for you?"

"Perfect. How 'bout we meet at the inn?"

"Okay. See you later."

"See you, buddy, and thanks."

"Hey, I'm always willing to meet for a free lunch," laughed Jun, sounding more like his usual self.

Pearce was relieved.

5

———

*a*t a rear table in the Tannersville Inn, Pierce sipped on his lemon water, waiting for Jun. When he arrived, Pierce stood up and waved him over. "Hi, Jun. Thanks for coming."

"Sure thing! It's good to see you." They shook hands, one arm hugged, and sat across from one another.

"How've you been, Jun? You look good."

"I'm fantastic, Howard. You look good too, and I see you haven't gotten fat in your retirement." He chuckled heartily.

"As you know, I married a great cook. Louise feeds me well, but not too well," he chuckled as well."

"I hear that. How is the missus?"

"She's good. Still teaches cooking lessons at Coral Bells. What about you? Seeing anyone?"

"I've been dating someone for the past few months," he grinned. "And get this, she shares my passion for guns. What are the odds?"

Pearce smiled. "Sounds like a match made in heaven."

"Right? Dallas is great."

"Dallas?"

Jun laughed. "Yeah. Great name, huh?"

"You don't meet many women named Dallas, that's for sure. I'm happy for you, pal."

"Thanks."

The waitress came over, and asked Jun, "Would you like anything to drink?"

"I'll have what he's having," he teased, recognizing Pierce wouldn't want to tempt him with a beer since he was still on duty.

"Sure," said the waitress, cheerfully. I'll be right back with your lemon water."

"And the girls, well, I hope?" asked Jun, reaching for the breadbasket.

"All good. Marie and her husband moved to California and are thriving in the balmy weather, and Jessie will be done with her master's at Columbia in a a few weeks. She's decided to stay in New York City where she assures us she'll land a job soon." Pierce sighed, missing his daughters.

"That's great, Howard. So tell me, how can I help you?" he asked, choosing a pumpernickel roll.

"We better order first before I get into it."

"I know what I'm having," said Leung, buttering the roll and taking a bite.

"Let me guess, a burger and fries," laughed Pierce.

"You got it."

"Some things never change."

"Hey, what can I say? I'm a creature of habit."

"I'll have the same, then. Don't wanna eat a salad watching you enjoy your lunch."

They both laughed, and Pierce signaled for the waitress.

After they ordered, Leung polished off the last of his roll. "That'll hold me 'till the burger comes." He sat back. "Ok, spill it. What's on your mind?"

"I've read the papers and interviewed the father. What I want to know is, have you guys kept anything from the public?"

Jun shook his head. "Sorry to say, there's nothing special about the case. As you may have read, there was no demand for ransom, a search in an around the premises ruled out foul play, and let's not forget, she left a note. That girl left home of her own volition."

"I agree, but what bothers me is that by leaving a note and not taking any personal belongings with her, other than what she was wearing, she probably meant to return home that day. So I wonder, what, or who detained her?"

Jun smiled wryly. "Are you really thinking this is another case where some random evidence will lead to an arrest, as in the Coral Bells case?"

Pierce shrugged. "The chances of that happening again are slim, but one thing I'm sure of is that girl meant to return home that day, and I need to find out why she didn't."

Jun scoffed, all traces of a smile disappearing. "Seriously, Sarge, the unit has been all over this. We interviewed the girl's family, school friends, neighbors, and anyone else who may have known her. Alibis have been double-checked, as well as finances and criminal records. You name it, we've covered it." He leaned back, reaching for his glass of water just as the waitress brought them their lunch, breaking the tension building between them.

"Will there be anything else?" she asked.

"No thank you," they both said.

When the waitress walked away, Pierce leaned in, "I don't doubt you guys are doing everything possible, Jun. Believe me, I know how diligent the detective squad works, especially when it comes to kids."

"Yeah well, believe me when I tell you, we understand the Robinsons' frustration. We feel it too, but with no new leads to follow, the case is officially cold, I'm sorry to say."

"I understand all too well how fast that happens. Tell me, who's in charge of the investigation?"

Jun grabbed the ketchup bottle and squeezed a few dollops over his fries. "Detective Robles. He came on board when Iggy left the unit."

"Is he approachable?"

Jun sucked in air. "Better not try. Nice enough guy, but strictly by the book."

Pearce frowned.

"Tell you what," Jun said, popping a french fry into his mouth. "I'll make copies of the file and meet you at Marty's after my shift at seven. You can buy me a few rounds, my friend."

"I'd be happy to. Thanks, buddy."

"No problem. Now, let me eat this burger so I can get back to work."

6

*P*ierce last visited Marty's Saloon in 2005, when his team surprised him to celebrate his remarkable investigation at the Coral Bells Senior Living Apartments. Initially, a tenant was presumed to have passed away due to natural causes, but Pierce uncovered a homicide.

Stepping inside the cop bar as it's known in the neighborhood, Pierce breathed in the familiar ambiance he did not realize he'd been missing. The too-loud music, louder conversations, and cigarette smoke permeating the room evoked a sense of nostalgia and belonging. He scanned the unfamiliar faces, searching for Jun.

A loud voice rang out. "Sarge!"

Pierce turned his head to where Jun waved enthusiastically. "Over here."

Mumbling apologies to a few people standing in his way, Pierce made it to Jun's table.

"I took the liberty of ordering a couple of cold ones when I saw you come in. Sit."

Pierce pulled out a chair and stared at the table, expecting an envelope.

Jun burst into laughter. "It's in the car. I didn't want these bozos to speculate about what I was giving to someone they may suspect is a snitch."

Pierce faked a laugh, bothered he may be mistaken for an informant, especially in his old stomping grounds.

"Thanks, I guess," he uttered sarcastically, but Jun had his eye on the barmaid coming their way.

"Hey, Sergeant Pierce, great to see you again," she said.

Forgetting his irritation when he recognized the barmaid, Pierce smiled, and said, "Hello, Mary."

"Nice to see you again, Sarge. How's retirement treating you?"

"I'm doing well, Mary," he replied, feeling a sense of relief that someone in the room full of fresh faces, still knew him.

"Glad to hear it." She set the beers down in front of them. "I'll be on the lookout for you guys in case you need anything else."

"Thanks, Mary," Pierce said.

Jun took a swallow of his beer and placed the mug down. "I reviewed the file before making copies for you. It's like I told you, there's nothing else we can do without a new lead."

"I'm sure you guys have done all you could, but perhaps a fresh pair of eyes will help find that girl. It will be worth the effort if only to reassure her parents that we haven't given up on finding their daughter."

Jun let out a deep sigh and grabbed his mug. He raised it in a toast towards Pierce, fully aware that his former boss was like a dog with a bone, refusing to let go once he began to dig his nose into an investigation with more questions than answers. "Here's to finding Maceen Robinson," Jun said, confident that Pierce would be the one to find the answers.

They clanked their mugs together.

After catching up and another round of beers, Pierce was

ready to head home. "Gotta go, buddy. Louise will be holding dinner for me." He signaled for Mary to bring the tab.

"We have to do this again. Next time I'll introduce you to Dallas."

"I'd like that."

At Jun's car, he gave Pierce the file. They shook hands, one arm hugged, and said their goodbyes.

On the way home, Pierce, grateful for the person he still had in the precinct to rely on, made a promise to himself—this would be the last time he would ask Jun for help. Jun meant the world to him, and he did not want to risk straining their friendship. The prospect of losing their bond would hurt.

7

Friday, March 19, 2010

*P*ierce carried out his good-luck ritual and ran his fingers over the company name etched on the door, and stepped inside. Frank and Ruby abruptly ended their conversation. "Frank, please follow me," announced Pierce, heading toward his private office. Frank flashed Ruby a knowing smile and leaped off the chair. From Pierce's demeanor and tone of voice, Frank and Ruby both sensed that a challenging investigation was about to commence—the type of case which Pierce excelled at and one that made their jobs exciting.

"Mr. Daniel Robinson has hired us to investigate the unexplained disappearance of his daughter, Maceen," remarked Pierce as soon as they were seated.

"Yeah," interrupted Frank. "Ruby and I figured you'd take that case."

"Nothing gets by you two," said Pierce, with a sly grin. "In any case, I'll need your assistance to re-interview some of the individuals associated with the girl. It's not going to be easy to solve this one. Too much time has passed since she was reported missing, but we're going to give it our all, aren't we?"

Frank nodded. "Yes, boss."

Pierce eyed Frank's stylish outfit—a polo shirt, skinny jeans, and Vans Old Skools sneakers. His hair was styled in the trendy teen cut, long on top and shorter at the sides and back.

He had already made the decision to involve Frank in the investigation, confident that Frank's ability to connect with young people would be a valuable initial step in unraveling this perplexing mystery. Meanwhile, Pierce would identify other individuals whom he intended to interrogate.

"Mr. Robinson said Maceen was a member of a hiking group. They meet most days after school at Yetter Park's Levee Loop for the four-and-a-half-mile walk."

Frank guessed where this conversation was heading, and while not happy with what he thought Pierce was about to ask of him, the chance to get involved in what may turn out to be a homicide intrigued him.

Pierce explained, "On weekends, they do a more arduous hike on various trails in the Poconos. The kids were scheduled to hike the two-hour red trail at Bushkill Falls on the morning of Maceen's disappearance. Mr. Robinson informed me that the police had discovered that Maceen bailed on the group the day before their hike because she had forgotten a dental appointment. She claimed that she wouldn't be able to hike after having a tooth pulled. However, the Robinsons pointed out that Maceen's claim of a dental appointment was false."

"Hmm," said Frank, "sounds like she had a secret boyfriend."

"According to Mr. Robinson, she did not have a boyfriend."

"Uh-huh, 'cause teenagers tell their parents everything," Frank snickered.

"Well, Frank, that's where you come in. I need you to infiltrate the group and see what you can find out about Maceen's disappearance. Think you can handle it?"

Even though he did not relish the idea of hiking, he couldn't bear the thought of missing out on the most thrilling case this office had ever encountered. "You bet," he replied enthusiastically.

Pierce ripped a sheet of paper from his notepad and offered it to Frank. "Here are the names of Maceen's hiking club members.

Frank reached for the list and tucked it in his pocket after giving it a quick glance.

"Be on the Levee Loop Trail this afternoon at three, so you don't miss them."

"How will I recognize them?"

Pierce pulled out a recent picture of the group he'd printed from their Facebook page and offered it to Frank.

"Here. This will help you identify them."

Frank peered at the photo of the smiling teens posing behind a trail marker that read, "Mile 8."

Frank gulped. "Eight miles? Those guys are serious!"

"Good thing you'll only be doing the Levee Loop, which is half the distance," Pierce said, trying to keep a straight face. "I'm sure you're up for it."

Frank smirked. "Do I need to get one of those fancy sunglasses like that tall guy in the picture is wearing? They look cool."

"Why not? However, it's important to remember that your primary objective is to charm them into letting you join the hike. Perhaps they'll share something useful that they didn't reveal to the police." Pierce flicked his hand towards Frank. "You know what to do."

This was not the first time Pierce had asked Frank to impersonate a teenager. With his boyish good looks and obsession with keeping up with the latest fads, twenty-eight-year-old Frank easily passed for a high schooler.

"I'll do my best," he chuckled. "But seriously, boss, after all this time, do you believe Maceen is still alive?"

Though he knew this was a possibility, Pierce responded, "It's not our job to guess, Frank. Our job is to find out what happened to her."

Frank nodded. "You can count on me."

"Don't worry too much about the assignment. Just be yourself and if you don't uncover anything beyond what the police have, at least we can rule them out for having anything to do with Maceen's disappearance."

Frank nodded. "Anything else?"

Pierce looked at his watch—9:45 a.m. "There's not much time for you to get ready. Better head home and study up on hiking the Appalachian Trail and what it takes to train for it."

Frank saluted, "Aye, aye," and dashed out the door.

As Pierce watched his assistant leave his office, he thanked his lucky stars he had taken a chance on hiring Frank Irizarry, a former security guard at the Coral Bells Adult Living Apartments. Although naïve and overenthusiastic, Frank exhibited a natural easy-going manner that got people talking. During the past two years, he'd proven his willingness to learn. Pierce thought ahead to the day he got tired of the game. With a couple more years under his belt, he was confident Frank Irizarry would be ready to take the reins and run the business without his guidance.

Pierce was certain that if Frank were accepted into the hiking group, he would come up with something useful to kickstart the investigation.

8

---

*A*s Ruby entered Pierce's office to bid him goodnight, he was bent over his desk, engrossed in his work, meticulously taking notes on his legal pad. "Have a pleasant evening," he said.

"Don't stay too late," cautioned Ruby, fully aware that once her boss got his hands on an intriguing case, he would not be able to get much rest until he solved it.

"I won't," he replied without raising his head.

Busy for much of the day juggling multiple cases and client meetings, the workday drew to a close before Pierce had the opportunity to go through Jun's folder.

Upon reviewing the paperwork, he examined his notes, highlighting and underlining certain words and making additional annotations.

— Maceen's 2007 grey, Jeep Wrangler found at the Martz Bus parking lot at Delaware Water Gap - doors locked, no foreign fingerprints.

— No one remembered Maceen at the bus ticket counter, in the parking lot, or on a bus, suggesting someone likely picked her up.

Who?

— No foul play evident, no ransom demand to get the FBI involved, or for police to apply for a warrant to obtain phone records.

— Her disappearance logged into the Pennsylvania National Missing Persons database and the National Missing and Unidentified Persons System.

— Nothing unusual found by police in her bedroom or in and around her home.

Recheck bedroom

— Interviewees: Parents, neighbors, students, teachers, friends, hiking club, employees and supervisors where Maceen and her friends were employed, Martz bus drivers, taxi dispatchers, and their drivers, owners of parked cars in the lot.

Who did they miss?

— Background checks of all persons interviewed.

No red flags.

Hiking club confirmed she canceled hike to Bushkill Falls on the day she disappeared because of a dental appointment. However, the parents confirmed that there was no dental appointment scheduled that week.

Where was she going???

Other interests Maceen may have besides hiking?

THREE HOURS after Ruby had gone home, Pierce dropped his pen and rubbed his eyes. He rolled back his chair, stretched his arms, and rubbed the back of his neck to alleviate the stiffness induced by bending over his desk.

Louise phoned, wanting to know when she might expect him. He promised to leave soon. That had been two hours ago.

Pierce grabbed the bathroom key from Ruby's desk and proceeded to the hallway outside his office to use the restroom. He stood over the sink, splashed cold water on his face and dried it with paper towels. After drying his face, he glanced at his watch. He was certain that Louise would understand if he stayed a little longer. *Just a bit longer.*

He needed to perk up and thought about brewing a pot of strong coffee to keep himself awake.

Standing before the open refrigerator door, holding a cold bottle of water, he contemplated Maceen's abrupt departure. Why did Maceen sneak out of the house? According to her father, Maceen always made sure to keep them updated on her whereabouts. If, as the lack of evidence indicating foul play suggests, and assuming no harm has befallen her, is there a secret boyfriend, as Frank suggested? And if so, is he responsible for her disappearance? *What were you up to, Maceen?*

Pierce's hand grew cold and cramped around the water bottle. He blinked and put it back into the refrigerator, closing the door softly. He'd begin fresh in the morning.

9

$\mathcal{E}$ xcited for today's undercover assignment, Frank spent most of the morning surfing the web. He was astounded by the substantial number of people expressing interest in undertaking a hiking expedition along the Appalachian Trail. Although the information intrigued him, Frank couldn't fathom why anyone would make such a grueling hike for fun. He thought these people were crazy.

Looking over the map of the Levee Loop trail, Frank decided the kids would likely begin the trek at the southeastern end of Dansbury Park, since they would be coming directly from school. A dirt path would lead them to the top of the Levee, where they would embark on their hike. Frank made a guess that they wouldn't choose the easternmost parking lot.

At 1:00 p.m., he shut down the computer and tuned into the local radio station. The morning had been chilly and windy, but Frank heard Joe Snedeker, the meteorologist, predict a warm and sunny day. He was so pumped to get started that he turned off the radio before the end of the forecast and jumped in the shower.

If Frank had listened to the entire forecast, he would have

learned that the summer weather Joe Snedeker had referred to was from the previous spring season. Today's forecast called for a partly cloudy day with temperatures expected to reach sixty degrees and wind gusts of up to ten miles per hour.

With enough time to reach the parking lot at Dansbury Park, Frank decided to indulge in his Call of Duty video game on his PlayStation 3, while eating a ham and cheese sandwich and a cup of coffee. Regularly checking his watch, he had to tear himself away from the game, leaving him little time to get ready.

In the absence of hiking boots, Frank resorted to a pair of worn-out combat boots he bought from the local Army Navy Store during his punk-rock phase. He then donned an old pair of sweatpants and a t-shirt.

He retrieved a bottle of water from the fridge and stuffed it into his backpack. Before dashing out the door, he grabbed a windbreaker hanging on a peg above his dumbbell rack.

As soon as Frank stepped outside, he realized his thin jacket failed to insulate him from the biting wind. He considered returning to his apartment to change into a warmer jacket, but when he glanced at his watch he sighed, realizing he should have double-checked the weather forecast before venturing out. He zipped up his windbreaker and sprinted to his car.

During the drive, Frank reviewed the research he had conducted on hiking and the numerous trails in the Poconos, particularly the Levee Loop Trail. He was confident that it would be a piece of cake to walk on the mostly flat and gravelly ground, with only slight inclines.

Upon arriving, Frank parked and followed the dirt path to the top of the levee where the trail began. While jogging in place, he blew on his chilled hands, eagerly anticipating the arrival of Maceen's friends. He kept checking his watch repeatedly.

As a couple holding walking sticks approached him, Frank, to avoid appearing suspicious, got into a stretching stance, imitating runners he'd seen in the park. After they had passed by, nodding their hellos, Frank commenced his hand-warming and stationary jogging.

Where are those kids?

Ten minutes later, he spotted a group of four walking up the path. He retrieved the photograph provided by Pierce from his wallet, and confirmed these were the members of Maceen's hiking club. *Show time!*

As the group drew nearer, Frank promptly tucked the photo into his pocket and fell in step with them.

"Excuse me," he greeted, putting on his friendliest smile, "Are you guys in training?"

"What's it to you?" replied a gangly, pimply-faced teen wearing aviator sunglasses.

"Nelson!" a pretty girl in cascading black braids, peeking out of her bucket hat, and down the front of her bright pink puffer jacket, and matching pants, cautioned, "Don't be rude."

Frank noticed the Appalachian Trail patch on Nelson's jacket and asked, "Does that patch mean you guys are going to hike the Appalachian Trail?" Without waiting for an answer, Frank eagerly shared his newfound knowledge. "I'm planning to be at Springer Mountain in the spring."

Nelson smirked. "You're gonna hike the Appalachian Trail from beginning to end?"

"Yup. Georgia to Maine. Any chance I can walk with you guys? It'd be cool to have some company."

Nelson opened his mouth, but before he could comment, the pretty girl in pink beat him to it.

"We're all training to hike the Appalachian Trail. You're welcome to join us." She moved closer to Frank. "Hi. I'm Jen."

"Nice to meet you, Jen. I'm Frank."

"Never seen you here before," she said.

Frank had anticipated the question. "I usually hike the Red

Rock Trail Loop to Mount Sophia. "It's peaceful and beautiful there. Ever hike it?"

"Is that in Cresco?" she asked.

"Yes."

"That's too far to travel for an after-school hike, but on Saturdays we do serious trails this side of the Poconos to build up our stamina. Some of those trails are as long as ten miles or more."

"No joke?" Frank blurted, sounding like an amateur. *Shit!*

Nelson sarcastically retorted. "Like Jen said, we have to keep our stamina up if we're going to be ready to tackle that monster trail next summer, so yeah, Frank, we hike for miles. Don't you?"

Frank met his eyes and confidently replied, "Of course."

"Uh-huh." Nelson gave Frank a measured look, and asked, "If you train in Cresco, what are you doing here?"

Stick to the script. "My mom's car broke down, and I had to drive her to work. Barely had enough time to make my first class. Dansbury Park is close to where she works, so I thought I'd squeeze in a walk around the Loop before picking her up."

"Do you live in Cresco?" asked Jen before Nelson had a chance to come up with another snide remark.

"No. Mount Pocono."

A gust of wind kicked up the leaves on the ground. It took all of Frank's willpower to ignore the goosebumps sprouting all over his body.

Jen looked Frank over. "Aren't you cold?"

"Are you kidding me? This weather's perfect for hiking."

Nelson scoffed. "Try to keep up then. We move at a pretty brisk pace."

"Yeah, man. Let's go," said Frank.

"C'mon gang." Nelson said to the team and began the trek.

"Don't pay him any mind. Nelson is protective of our little group," whispered Jen.

"Sure, I get it," Frank replied.

"The weekend is the only time we have to do a real hike," she said, quickening her pace. "During the week, we train here after school before going to work. Everyone except Oliver." Jen tilted her head to the side, where a teen sporting an afro sticking out the sides of his cap, wearing the same jacket with the Appalachian Trail patch as Nelson, and sporting the same aviator glasses, lagged behind. "He doesn't have a job," Jen said, her voice dropping to a whisper. "He studies a lot, *a lot!* He's going to Harvard," she added with a wide smile.

Oliver had been enjoying the exchange between Nelson and Frank, but at the mention of his name, he called out, "I heard that, Jen."

Frank turned toward Oliver. "Harvard? Impressive."

"You see, Jen? He's impressed," exclaimed Oliver with a cocky smile.

"The fourth hiker in the group, barely a head shorter than Frank's six feet, with long, thin legs wearing tan and white leggings, a chocolate-colored sweater jacket, and a wide head-band, had been silent until now. She introduced herself, saying "And I'm Cindy."

"Yes, sorry Cindy," Jen said.

"Nice to meet you all," said Frank.

Nelson looked over his shoulder. "Pick up the pace, will ya?" he yelled.

Frank considered himself in good shape, lifting weights at home at least three times a week. Running, walking or hiking was not something he considered doing, but he thought in his physical condition, this hike wouldn't be a problem for him.

Observing the group, he struggled to hold back his laughter at the way they pumped their arms and took quick steps while rolling their feet from heel to toe.

Despite feeling somewhat embarrassed, he mimicked the

group's stance and hastily approached Oliver, intending to bring up Maceen and how she fit into the group.

"Hey Oliver ..."

"We don't talk during training, man," said Oliver without breaking stride.

Damn! These guys are serious.

After twenty minutes, the wind died down, and clouds finally gave way to the sun. Frank unzipped his jacket. A few minutes later, one by one of his companions removed their outer garments, stowed their hats in their pockets, and tied the sleeves around their waists. Frank noticed that they did not seem bothered by the hanging coats brushing against their legs as they continued their peculiar gait.

The four-and-a-half-mile trail finally came to an end, Frank looking a bit worse for wear, his red and sweaty face a testament to his lack of training. Just as he thought he would finally be able to mention Maceen, Nelson announced, "All right, team, stretch out and hydrate before our next go-around." Frank gulped down his water bottle, knowing he wouldn't be doing that again.

"Don't you guys need to be at work?" Frank asked, trying to control his breathing. "Jen said you all have jobs, uh, except for Oliver."

Nelson, eyeing Frank suspiciously, said, "We have plenty of time to do another round."

If Frank were ever to do some investigative work, he thought now would be the time. He jumped right in.

"Have there always been just the four of you in this group?" he asked.

Nelson stopped stretching and asked, "Why do you want to know that?"

"I remember reading about a missing girl who was training to hike the Appalachian Trail, that's all. Was she part of this group?"

Everyone froze, their eyes fixed on Nelson, except for Oliver who looked uneasy and kept his eyes downcast.

Interesting.

"Maceen. She was a member of our group," Cindy replied, beating Nelson to the punch.

"Oh wow. Any idea what happened to her?"

"Of course not, Frank," snapped Nelson. The police don't even know what happened to her."

"No need to get upset, man. I was only asking."

"Let's just finish stretching, all right?"

An uncomfortable silence enveloped the teens as they stretched, their eyes fixed on the ground, avoiding Frank's gaze.

Frank thought it best to cool it with the questions for now, and kept his eye on them. He imitated their stretching routine, and noticed Oliver giving him the side-eye. *What's with him?*

After a few minutes, Nelson, announced, "Let's go, guys."

Frank's mind was racing with the urgency of finding a way out of this situation.

"Oh shit," Frank cried, looking at his watch, "I promised to run an errand for my mom before picking her up. If you guys are hiking tomorrow, can I meet up with you?"

Nelson blew out a breath. "Are you sure you're up for this, Frank? You don't strike me as a serious hiker." He pointed at Frank's feet with a smirk. "And you don't even have the proper footwear."

Frank wasn't going to let Nelson embarrass him. He knew how to handle a smart-alecky attitude.

He let his shoulders sag, putting on his saddest face, and sighed. "These combat boots belonged to my dad. He was killed in Vietnam."

Jen gasped and bowed her head. Oliver avoided eye contact. Cindy cast Nelson a sly glance. Frank thought she was enjoying Nelson's discomfort.

"Oh man, I'm so sorry," Nelson mumbled.

"Sorry," the group chorused.

Frank explained. "I do have hiking boots, but today's my dad's birthday. To honor him, I decided to wear his boots."

Nelson's face flushed red and he shuffled his feet, wanting to run away.

Okay. One more lie to seal the deal, thought Frank.

Addressing Nelson, Frank explained. "Look, I know I'm not in hiking shape right now, but I had an appendectomy a couple of weeks ago. My doctor said to take it easy for a while, but I've already wasted enough time being sick, so I thought I'd get back to training. I didn't mean to slow you guys down."

He caught a glimpse of Cindy, and there it was again—that mischievous smile behind her eyes. *Oh yeah, she's thoroughly enjoying his embarrassment.*

Everyone stared at Nelson wide-eyed.

"No ... man," replied Nelson with a slight stutter. "Don't sweat it. We'll help you prepare for the Appalachian Trail." He turned to the group. "Won't we, guys?"

Everyone nodded in agreement. "Yeah, for sure," Jen said. "If you're certain you're up to it, meet us at the Lake Lenape parking lot tomorrow morning."

"I'll be there," said Frank, faking enthusiasm. "What time?"

"Eight. Know where that is?"

"Sure."

Nelson forced a smile. "Great, we're planning to hike Mount Minsi, so make sure you wear your hiking boots."

Once again, Jen wasn't able to suppress her startled gasp.

Nelson cocked his head toward her and added, "I meant the trail is pretty rocky, so it's important to wear appropriate footwear, *Jen.*"

The group began to fidget, staring between Nelson and Frank as if watching a tennis match.

Had Frank not detected Nelson's subtle dig behind his feeble smile, he would not have uttered, "Don't worry about me,

Nelson. These boots were made for hiking. If not, the U.S. Army would not issue them to soldiers who do more hiking than we're ever going to do," but he couldn't help himself.

Nelson's face turned from a fiery red to a pale ashen.

"Okay, Frank, catch you tomorrow," Jen chimed in, saving Nelson from another stupid blunder. "Get there early. The parking lot fills up fast on the weekends."

"Will do. See you tomorrow, and thanks for letting me hike with you all."

On the drive home, Frank worried about doing a more strenuous hike than the one he had just put his poor body through, but he had nothing to report, and he was determined not to let Pierce down.

10

A gentle hand shook his shoulder, jolting him awake from a deep sleep.

"Wake up Howie, Ruby's on the phone," Louise softly said.

Pierce croaked, "What time is it?"

"Nine-thirty, and before you ask, I turned off the alarm to let you sleep in. You looked like hell when you came in last night."

Pierce cleared his dried throat. "Thanks, hon, but I might've missed a meeting this morning, probably why Ruby's calling."

Louise clicked her tongue. "Meetings can be rearranged."

She bent over him and kissed his forehead. "Don't keep Ruby waiting," she admonished, and left the bedroom.

Pierce slipped his feet into his slippers and made his way to the den, where he picked up the phone.

"Good morning, Ruby. Sorry to keep you waiting. What'd I miss?"

"Morning, boss. You had a nine-thirty with Mr. Yang, a new client, who suspects an employee of stealing."

"Sorry, Ruby. I overslept. Please apologize for me and postpone to a later time."

"Not to worry. I waited until eight forty-five, then called Mr. Yang to reschedule."

"Whatever would I do without you, Ruby? You're a peach."

They both giggled at his endearing compliment.

"Anything else on the agenda this morning?"

"A couple of meetings, but if you're not coming in, I can rearrange those too."

"If you can squeeze them in for this afternoon, I should be in no later than one. I'll ring you if I don't make it by then."

"Will do. See you later, boss."

"Bye, Ruby."

Pierce ran his fingers through his tousled hair and let out a loud yawn, contemplating giving the Robinsons a call.

He flipped through his notepad on the desk, found the phone number, and dialed.

A woman's shaky voice answered. "Hello?"

"Mrs. Robinson?"

"Yes."

"I'm Howard Pierce. Your husband hired me to look into …"

"Yes," she interrupted. "I know who you are."

"I was wondering if I may drop by this morning."

"Have you any news?" she asked, expectantly.

Pierce sensed the desperation in her voice and responded gently, "No, ma'am. I simply want to meet with you and Mr. Robinson to familiarize myself with Maceen's surroundings.

Silence ensued.

After a brief moment, Pierce asked, "Mrs. Robinson? Is this morning convenient for you?"

"Yes, yes, of course," she said impatiently.

Pierce glanced at the wall clock. "I can be there at eleven. Will that be all right?"

"Eleven is fine. Goodbye, Mr. Pierce."

"Goodbye, Mrs. Robinson. See you then."

Pierce blew out a breath. *Better get ready.*

Freshly showered and shaved, Pierce enjoyed an omelet with a side of Canadian bacon, toast, orange juice, and two cups of coffee. Louise was determined not to let her husband out of the house with his usual promise to pick something up on his way out, a bad habit he acquired while the lead investigator at the police department. Ensuring that he ate every bite, Louise sat across from him while nursing a cup of coffee.

———

RESIDING PREDOMINANTLY in the Poconos for most of his life, with the exception of the four years he dedicated to earning his bachelor's degree in criminology at York College, Pierce lamented the peaceful sounds of the surrounding woods that had been replaced by the construction noise of the newly developed communities springing up all over the Poconos.

To the right of the Robinson residence, an unoccupied plot of land displayed a for-sale sign featuring the builder's familiar logo and contact information. A majestic pine, oak, and birch tree stood tall on the plot, and he couldn't help but feel a sense of sadness that these beautiful trees would soon be cut down.

Next to the lot stood a two-story, brick house where Chino Martinez, and his young family, resided for the last five years. They welcomed Daniel Robinson and his family when they moved in, and the two families quickly became close friends. Pierce disregarded Martinez as a possible suspect after reviewing his background check and the police report.

The house to the left of the Robinsons lacked any windows or doors. Coincidentally, a truck loaded with these materials pulled onto the premises.

Pierce watched them unload for a minute and then turned

his attention across the street. Busy spreading hay on his recently sowed lawn, Mr. Alex Patel was surprised by his toddler who came running out of the house, followed by his mother. He picked up his son and brought him back to his mom with a kiss and a hug. The parents gave each other a peck on the cheek, and Patel watched his family walk up the narrow path to her parked car. He waved to them until they drove away.

According to the file Jun gave Pierce, the lot where the Patel house currently stands had a for-sale sign when Maceen disappeared.

Patel spotted Pierce and gave him a friendly wave. Pierce waved back and watched Patel spread hay across his soon-to-be-lawn, picking up where he had left off. Pierce reflected on how challenging and expensive it would be to grow grass over the many rocks and boulders underneath much of the terrain in the Poconos.

Mr. Josef Schmidt, a widower, occupied the house adjacent to the Patels. Mr. Schmidt had been out of town the day Maceen went missing, returning home late that evening.

On the gravel driveway leading to the Robinson's front door, Pierce couldn't help but admire the well-kept landscaping. The property was spotless, with no debris in sight. New plantings of lambs ear, spicebush, and hostas blended seamlessly with a few unfamiliar shrubs. Someone must have warned the Robinsons of the rocks beneath the soil, as they had chosen to landscape their property with vibrant bushes and newly planted trees, and carefully arranged stones. Pierce thought this created a more natural environment.

He took a deep breath and rang the doorbell, ready to interview the Robinsons.

11

*a*t the door, a woman wearing jeans, a light blue sweater, and slippers, whom Pierce presumed to be Mrs. Robinson, greeted him. She displayed a smile that contrasted with the sadness in her eyes.

When he stepped inside, she gently remarked, "I'll take your jacket."

Pierce slipped it off and handed it to her. "Thank you."

She hung his jacket in the nearby closet. "Please take off your shoes and leave them on the mat." She pointed to where two pairs of slippers were neatly arranged. "You may wear slippers if you wish."

Pierce stared at the two pairs and thought neither would fit his feet.

He bent down to untie his shoelaces and remove his shoes, feeling gratitude for his wife's warning about wearing worn-out socks or ones with holes.

Mrs. Robinson watched him patiently as he carefully placed his shoes next to the slippers. When he stood, she ushered him into the living room. "Please, get comfortable while I go find my husband. He's out back."

Pierce watched her slip her socked feet into backless sneakers near the sliding doors and step outside, quietly closing the door behind her.

The elegant blend of Japanese and American decor, characterized by its subtle color scheme and harmonious wooden accents, captivated his attention. A few plants basked in the sun on the spacious window sill. He surmised that the ornate wooden cabinet with double doors concealed a television set. An array of family pictures adorned the mantle's stone fireplace.

As Pierce was admiring the photographs, Daniel Robinson entered the room, followed by his wife who quietly closed the sliding door shut. The couple promptly removed their shoes and arranged them neatly on the mat. Clad in their slippers, Mrs. Robinson headed to the kitchen while Daniel greeted Pierce.

"Good morning, Mr. Pierce," said Daniel with a friendly handshake. "Please have a seat while Sakura prepares coffee for you."

Pierce noticed the bags under his eyes and a slight tremor when they shook hands.

"Thank you," Pierce said, settling on the sofa, "But please don't trouble yourselves."

Robinson took a seat on the loveseat opposite him. "No trouble at all. My wife insists."

"You have a beautiful home, Mr. Robinson."

"I appreciate your kind words. However, I must give credit to my wife. She has a preference for simplistic and open spaces, which aligns with the principles of feng shue. Although I must admit, I am not an expert in this area." He offered a faint smile.

"It's better to let our wives handle the decorating, they're more skilled at it than we are."

"Yes," agreed Daniel.

Pierce deemed it prudent to keep up the chitchat until Mrs. Robinson could join them, in order to get a sense of the couples' interaction. He commented, "Lots of new construction going on around here."

"Indeed!"

"Been living here long?"

"My wife and I bought this property a number of years ago, as our retirement home. However, we made the decision to have a house built and relocate to the Poconos when our community began to change."

"How so?"

Before he could answer, Mrs. Robinson entered the room carrying a white, lacquered tray intricately decorated with colorful lanterns. A carafe, small pitcher of cream, sugar bowl, and a cup and saucer with a small spoon were neatly arranged, accompanied by a small plate of cookies and cloth napkins. With meticulous care, she placed the tray beside Pierce on the floral ottoman table and poured the coffee. "Would you like cream and sugar, Mr. Pierce?" she asked politely.

"No, thank you, black is fine. And please, call me Howard."

"Help yourself to cookies," she said, ignoring his request for familiarity. Holding the saucer delicately, she offered him the coffee. When he accepted, she walked around the table and sat next to her husband.

"Mr. Pierce was just asking what made us decide to move here," Daniel said, turning to face his wife.

"For several reasons, our peaceful and safe neighborhood in Harrison, New Jersey, transformed into a crowded and noisy place with all the new high-risers going up to accommodate commuters. So, in the summer of 2008 when the house was finished, we decided to move to the Poconos."

Pierce, who typically takes notes during interviews, decided against it since he had already read the case file. Some of the questions he was about to ask, were already answered, but he wanted to observe their reactions. He explained, "I asked to see you both because I'm interested in learning more about Maceen."

They glanced at one another. "What do you mean?" asked Daniel.

For instance, "How did the move affect your daughter? Not many teens want to get uprooted away from their friends."

"Your coffee's getting cold, Mr. Pierce," warned Sakura.

"Howard, please."

Sakura nodded politely.

Pierce took a sip of the aromatic coffee, and although he wasn't in the mood, took one of the small cookies and popped it in his mouth. "This cookie is delicious, Mrs. Robinson, thank you."

"I'm pleased you like it. It's my mother's recipe," she said without smiling.

Daniel was aware his wife found it difficult to talk about their daughter and was making an effort to steer away from the subject. He cleared his throat. "To answer your question, Howard, we had been vacationing in the Poconos since Maceen was a little girl. She loved it here, so it wasn't hard to convince her."

"Maceen was a junior in high school when you moved out here. Why didn't you wait another year so she could graduate with her classmates?"

Pierce noticed the couple appeared uneasy with his question, as they both avoided making eye contact with him.

With a heavy heart, Daniel shared that their daughter was being bullied by a group of girls.

Pierce asked, "Do you know why?"

Sakura, trying to control her emotions, explained, "I think it was because they were racist towards a half-Irish, half-Japanese girl."

Daniel looked uncomfortable at his wife's bluntness.

"I'm sorry to hear that," said Pierce. "Was it verbal abuse, or did it escalate to physical abuse?"

Daniel, fearing his wife might lose her composure and get angry when she recalled her daughter's abuse, replied, "There was some pushing and shoving when she passed them in the hallways, but it was mainly verbal."

"I assume the school was informed."

Sakura responded, impatiently, "Yes, of course, but teachers aren't everywhere."

"Did you check Maceen's phone bill for any unrecognized numbers?"

Daniel replied, "Yes, we did go through her phone bill after she went missing, but apart from calls between her best friend, Cindy, work-related, and home calls, we didn't find any unknown numbers on her bill. Of course that was before ..." He lowered his head. "Nothing since then."

"Did Maceen keep in touch with any of her friends from Jersey?"

"While she had friends, some since kindergarten, a few kept in touch for a while, but as time went on, they simply lost touch," Sakura answered.

"Apart from her hiking group companions, did Maceen form friendships with others, perhaps a best friend?"

Sakura nodded, and in a lighter tone, said, "In fact, her best friend, Cindy, is the one who encouraged her to join the hiking group ..."

"And Oliver," chimed in Daniel. "He's her study buddy, when they're not out hiking."

"Yes, Oliver. He's Harvard-bound," Sakura proudly said.

"So other than the ones in the hiking group, she has no other friends?" Pierce persisted.

"Unlike some young people who like to hang out, Maceen's studies take up a lot of her free time, Mr. Pierce," Sakura retorted, anger creeping into her voice.

At this point, Pierce began to grasp the dynamics of this couple. While both were struggling with the situation, Daniel demonstrated a willingness to cooperate. In contrast, Sakura responded by avoiding answering questions she didn't want to answer, or letting out her frustration in anger.

"Howard, please."

Sakura, once again disregarded his invitation to address him by his first name. She remarked, "Hiking with her group is the one social activity she never misses," hoping to put an end to the matter of Maceen's social life.

"And that's because they have a goal Maceen shares," Daniel added.

"Yes, to hike the Appalachian Trail," said Pierce.

"Precisely."

Although Daniel had answered the question of boys during his interview with Pierce, Pierce wanted to hear from Sakura. "What about boys? Did she have a boyfriend, or did she go out on dates?"

Sakura looked away, letting out an exasperated breath.

"Of course, boys were interested. She's a beautiful girl," said Daniel, "but like Sakura said, our girl is serious about her studies. She knows there's time for dating once she finishes her education." Tears sprang to his eyes. "Recently, our precious daughter turned eighteen. We had planned to surprise her by letting her pick out a new car." He cleared his throat. "That old Jeep isn't going to last much longer," he softly said.

Sakura choked back a sob.

Pierce was aware Maceen had turned eighteen on February 4th, and understood that if he found her alive and well, the decision of her return home would now fall upon her as an adult.

He finished his coffee and leaned over to put the cup and saucer on the tray. He picked up the napkin, dabbed his mouth, and continued the interview.

"Did either of you notice a change in your daughter's routine the days or weeks before she went missing?"

The Robinsons reached for each other's hand. Sakura's eyes watered.

"I apologize for bringing up these questions, but knowing your daughter's habits and any deviations from them may help me locate her."

"We understand," Daniel replied. "I don't recall anything out of the ordinary."

He turned toward his wife. "What about you, sweetheart, did you notice any changes in Maceen's behavior, no matter how slight?"

She shook her head. "No, nothing."

"I understand she left before either of you were up. Was it unusual for the hiking group to meet before dawn?"

Sakura sighed. "Maceen had never left the house before we woke up. I suppose leaving a note instead of informing us of her plans the night before is unusual, but we trust her," she emphasized. "We believed the group decided on an earlier hike, possibly because the trail was further than the ones they had been hiking. She simply forgot to tell us."

Pierce addressed Daniel. "During our interview you mentioned that Maceen told the group she had a dental appointment and wasn't able to go on the hike ..."

Sakura swallowed another sob.

Daniel admitted, "Yes, Cindy informed us. But Maceen had never lied to us before. We fear someone forced her to leave home and lied to her group and to us."

Pierce understood the parents were unable to accept Maceen's deception and were clinging to the notion that she left home involuntarily.

"It doesn't do any good to speculate why Maceen left home earlier than usual. There might be a simpler explanation that we haven't thought of yet. I promise you both, I will do my best to find out what happened to your daughter."

Daniel offered a weak smile. Sakura turned away to wipe away a tear.

Pierce realized Mrs. Robinson wouldn't be able to withstand his questions much longer, but he wanted to be sure he covered everything. He plowed on.

"Is there anything else that seemed out of the ordinary surrounding that day?"

Sakura fidgeted. Daniel lowered his head and touched his forehead.

"Now that I think about it, that evening I noticed the floodlights did not automatically turn on when I returned from reporting her," he swallowed, "missing. I checked the circuit breaker box, and to my dismay, I found that the floodlights had been switched off."

Pierce interpreted this as another indication that Maceen planned her getaway.

"Do you remember what time you both got up that day?"

Daniel opened his mouth to speak, but Sakura cut him off. "During the week, I get up at six to say goodbye to Daniel before he takes the bus into the city. He'll pick up something to eat there. Maceen and I have breakfast together before she goes to school. That leaves me plenty of time to make it to my kindergarten class. On the weekends, I rise at seven, so yes, I got up at seven that Saturday."

"And that's when you found her note?"

Sakura blinked. "Yes."

"Neither of you has ever been contacted by anyone with information about Maceen's whereabouts. Correct?"

"That's correct," said Daniel.

Pierce gave them a moment and asked his next question.

"Have you or any of her friends heard from Maceen since she left home?"

Sakura spoke up. "Don't you think we would have informed the police if she had contacted her friends or us?"

Daniel patted her arm. "Mr. Pierce has to ask these questions, sweetheart."

"No one has contacted us since she left home. Despite her friends' calls and texts, especially Cindy's, she hasn't responded. We call her daily but she doesn't answer our calls either," Daniel replied, gently rubbing his wife's arm.

"Do you believe Maceen deactivated the circuit to prevent the headlights from startling you as she drove away?" Pierce inquired, keeping his gaze on Daniel.

"I suppose so, but honestly," he averted his eyes, "I forgot about the lights when the police came to the house."

"That's understandable."

Daniel mustered a wry smile.

"Had she ever done a hike by herself?"

"Oh no," answered Daniel, shaking his head. "We would not have been comfortable letting her hike alone. As my wife mentioned, Maceen was introduced to the sport by Cindy. She likes a challenge and enjoys the activity as well as her new friends. She would never have attempted to hike without them."

"I'm aware the police conducted a search of Maceen's bedroom but found no valuable information to aid in their investigation. With your permission, I would like to have a look at her bedroom."

"What do you mean?" Daniel asked. Sakura stared at Pierce, wide-eyed.

"Observing her personal space will give me a better understanding of your daughter than reading a police report."

Sakura objected, saying, "We already told you what kind of girl she is."

"Yes, ma'am, and I appreciate that, but by examining her bedroom, I may gain a different perspective than what is in the police report. I promise not to disturb anything."

Sakura turned toward her husband for support. When he didn't react, she spoke in a weary voice, "Daniel, would you please escort Mr. Pierce up to Maceen's bedroom?"

Daniel promptly stood. "Please follow me."

12

On the second level of the house, Daniel turned the doorknob, pushed open Maceen's bedroom door, and stepped aside. "Give a shoutout if you need me," he said, and swiftly descended the staircase.

Pierce stood at the entrance, looking around the tidy room. After months of Maceen's disappearance, someone, most likely her mother, routinely dusted and vacuumed, anticipating her daughter's return.

In addition to the posters adorning the wall of The Blackeye Peas, Taylor Swift, and Kings of Leon, Maceen had tacked on a large map of the Appalachian Trail to the remaining wall space.

On her desk, neatly stacked, were books on math, history, botany, and a worn copy of *To Kill A Mocking Bird*. Pierce picked up each book, holding it by the front and back covers. Given Maceen's careful planning and successful getaway, he didn't expect anything to fall out, but he shook the books wanting to be sure. He picked up a framed picture of a smiling Maceen, on a hiking trail with her friends. Pierce took the frame apart but found no hidden note. He put it back together and carefully placed it where he had found it. The remaining desk space was occupied by a school binder. He leafed through it and found nothing suspicious; merely schoolwork.

The computer had already been searched by the police, but Pierce moved the mouse to see if it would open. The password screen came on. He shrugged and made sure everything on the desk was as it was before.

A trough-style planter brimming with greenery, soaking up the sunlight that peeked through the blinds, caught his eye. Pierce gently touched the damp soil and felt a pang of sadness for Maceen's parents who were taking care of the plant in her absence. Staring at the window box reminded him of one of his cases as a homicide detective. During a search of the suspect's premises, Pierce discovered bullets buried in flower pots filled with live evergreens. He did not expect Maceen to have hidden bullets in the soil, *but,* he thought, *you never know.* However, he decided not to disturb the plantings.

Activating his cell phone's camera, he took a picture before carefully lifting the planter to examine its underside. A faintly legible telephone number had been meticulously penciled. He set the planter down and pulled out his pad, scribbling down the number.

Subsequently, his attention was drawn to the bedside table, draped in a white linen cloth that matched the duvet on the bed. The table had no drawers to search. He moved the lamp and alarm clock to one side, peeked under the table cloth, and then inspected the lamp and alarm clock before putting everything back to its original place. Pierce then bent down to examine the area under the bed and in between the mattresses. He ran his hand over the back of the headboard and smoothed out the bed covers.

Pierce did a thorough examination of the dresser drawers, carefully running his hand in and around Maceen's clothing, and sticking his hands in her bobby socks. The only thing he found on the shelf in her closet was a heavy quilt, which he unfolded and shook out. Before neatly refolding the quilt and putting it back as he found it, he ran his hand carefully over the shelf. Pierce rummaged through every pocket of her garments, and through the small pockets of her empty book bag hanging on a hook in the closet, but found nothing hidden. He inspected a pair of sneakers, loafers, and slippers diligently searching for any concealed note that might be hidden within.

The search yielded no evidence of a diary—No contraceptives, drugs, trinkets, hidden pictures, or love letters.

After taking one last look around to see if he'd missed anything, he took a few more pictures of the entire room, turning his body to capture every angle.

The Robinsons were quietly talking when Pierce walked into the living room. "Thank you for letting me see Maceen's bedroom," he announced.

The couple abruptly stood.

"Did you find anything to help you, Howard?" Daniel asked expectantly.

"Perhaps. Was Maceen interested in botany?"

"Why do you ask?"

"I noticed a plant on her windowsill and a book titled *Alpines and Bog Plants* on her desk."

Realizing the interview was not yet over, they sat. Pierce did the same.

Daniel thought for a moment and said, "Perhaps the book may have been assigned by her science teacher, although Maceen borrows library books on a variety of topics that interest her."

Daniel turned toward his wife. "She didn't say she wanted to cultivate plants though, did she Sakura?"

Sakura shook her head. "No, she never said."

"Was the plant on her window sill a gift, or did she buy it?"

Sakura raised her voice more than she had intended. "What does her plant have anything to do with her disappearance?"

Daniel reached for her hand.

"Perhaps nothing," Pierce answered, "but you never know when a minor detail might lead to a clue."

Mr. Robinson turned toward his wife, whose brow was wrinkled. She couldn't comprehend Pierce's logic. "I'm sure Mr. Pierce knows what he's doing," he said.

Sakura inhaled deeply, tightened her grip of Daniel's hand, and said, "Maceen bought the plant. She claimed it was a science project. I believe she was attempting to grow cranberries or some such fruit."

Pierce thought it was an unusual choice but kept it to himself. "I see," he remarked.

Daniel began to fidget. Sakura sighed." I apologize for my outburst, Mr. Pierce," not sounding at all remorseful.

"No need. I understand how stressful this is for you both."

Sakura began to tap her foot, wishing he would stop asking questions and go away.

But Pierce wasn't finished. "You said Maceen studied at the library. Did she go there every day after school?"

"Most days except Friday and Saturday evenings when she was at work," replied Daniel.

"My daughters also loved to study in the library where it's quiet," said Pierce, hoping to lighten the mood.

A fleeting smile crossed Daniel's lips. Sakura stared, expressionless.

"Yes, like my wife said, she studies with her classmate, Oliver." Daniel chuckled, in a momentary relief from his grief. "They're two of a kind when it comes to getting into college."

Pierce continued describing his search of their daughter's bedroom. "A brief search of your daughter's dresser and closet revealed no useful information."

Sakura stiffened, her face blanched. "You went through her drawers?" she asked.

"Mrs. Robinson, in my experience teens hide things from their parents. I was simply being thorough."

Sakura's eyes narrowed.

Pierce explained, "In searching her belongings, I didn't necessarily expect to find illicit substances. It is possible that finding something trivial, like a Valentine's Day card, or a note, could provide a clue to a person of interest or their whereabouts on that day. Even a trinket given to her by someone could lead us closer in uncovering the truth behind Maceen's disappearance."

"And did you find anything?" she asked, her eyes gleaming with hope.

"No, ma'am, nothing of that sort."

Sakura pursed her lips, and nodded her head.

Pierce, wanting to avoid further upsetting the grieving parents, decided to end the interview. He stood up and said, "Thank you both for your hospitality."

Mr. Robinson held his coat while Pierce bent to tie the laces of his shoes. Sakura had said goodbye in the living room and retreated to the backyard, her anger rising at Pierce's intrusion into her daughter's things, only to find nothing that could aid in finding her daughter.

"My investigation may take some time, and I can't promise I'll find Maceen, but I'll do my best," Pierce said.

"I appreciate that," said Daniel, giving Pierce a firm handshake.

Driving away, Pierce pondered his impressions of Maceen's parents and what he gleaned from their daughter's spotless bedroom.

———

As the day wore on, Pierce found himself growing increasingly fatigued. It was only after he had completed his other tasks and met with Mr. Yang, whom Ruby had rescheduled from this morning, that he was able to refocus on the Maceen investigation. With his eyes closed and reclining in his office chair, Pierce reviewed the information gathered thus far.

He understood why, despite the comprehensive investigation by the detective squad, the case had swiftly deteriorated into a cold case due to the absence of any new information.

The interview with the Robinsons and the search of Maceen's bedroom strengthened his belief that Maceen left her house willingly. Sneaking out before her parents awoke, turning off the floodlights, and lying to her friends and family, indicated she had a plan.

Sitting up, Pierce steepled his fingers and gazed upon the chaotic array of papers with scribbled notes and hasty reminders strewn across his desk, revealing a complex case.

With the enigmatic telephone number on his mind, he recalled the police statement from a Mr. Schmidt, a retiree living across the street from the Robinsons. Pierce reached for Jun's copy of the case file and found the statement in which the neighbor asserted to have been visiting his son in Ohio the day Maceen left home. The concealed number beneath the planter did not prove Maceen, or someone she knew, had written it, but a telephone number with an Ohio area code, and a neighbor whose son lived in Ohio? That's a coincidence he couldn't ignore. He wondered if that hidden telephone number held the key to finding her.

Although concerned that his 570 area code might give away his location and alert someone involved in Maceen's disappearance, Pierce took a chance and dialed. After six rings, the automated message to leave a number came on. Pierce hung up, pushed back his chair, and began to pace.

The botany book in Maceen's bedroom while innocuous, its existence troubled Pierce. One, because her parents claimed not to be aware of her interest in botany, and two, since the book was not borrowed from the library, it was likely suggested by someone who convinced Maceen to read up on the subject. Was that same someone the person she snuck out of her house to meet?

Why did Maceen leave home? Was it because of a boyfriend, a parent, or abuse? The Robinsons admitted their daughter had been abused in school before they moved to the Poconos. Did she face abuse here as well? Maceen intended to return home, of that he was certain. What or who prevented her from doing so? His mind was filled with questions.

Pierce abruptly stopped pacing and plopped down in his chair.

He grabbed the computer mouse and began a search at the East Stroudsburg High School website. While the study of photosynthesis and ecosystems was offered in their science program, botany, per se, was not a requisite or elective.

Mrs. Robinson mentioned her daughter was trying to grow cranberries.

Pierce researched methods for cultivating cranberries indoors. It made sense that someone with experience had initiated germination and planted the seeds before presenting the planter to Maceen.

Cranberries grow in bogs. Oh no!

An internet search of the Tannersville Cranberry Bog revealed that its deepest point is approximately sixty feet. *If that poor girl's body has been disposed of there, she will never be found.*

Pierce set aside that thought and concentrated on what he did know. He repeatedly tapped a pencil on his desk, reflecting on the challenges he faced while investigating the teen's mysterious disappearance months after the incident. Despite the difficulties, he remained determined to unravel the mystery and make sense of it all.

Long after Ruby had gone home, Pierce was still mulling over the files. He wanted to interview the widower, living across the street from the Robinsons, the following day, but Louise had plans for them to spend the day in the town of Jim Thorpe, looking for antiques and relaxing over dinner and a glass of wine —her way of making Pierce relax.

It'll have to wait 'til next week, he sighed.

His stomach began to rumble. He checked the time and realized that he had been in the office for a couple of hours after quitting time. He stretched and let out a big yawn. *Okay, time to go home. I'm famished.*

He turned off the lights and locked the office door.

13

Saturday, March 20, 2010

Frank arrived at the Lake Road parking lot a half hour early, his mind racing with anxiety for the upcoming hike. The sleepless night had left him feeling jittery and on edge. He turned on the news and listened to the weather forecast in its entirety. He was not about to get caught under-dressed again.

However, determined not to embarrass himself this time, he stretched his stiff limbs, ate a filling breakfast, and downed two aspirins before leaving his apartment. He had thought of everything except to carry nothing but water in his backpack.

A few minutes later, Frank spotted the teens exiting Nelson's car. He casually leaned on his vehicle, one foot crossed over the other, with one arm over the roof as he'd seen the cool kids do in the movies.

Nelson noticed Frank when he slammed his car door shut and waved.

Frank nodded.

The group, led by their leader approached. As anticipated, the parking lot began filling up shortly thereafter.

"Hi, Frank. Glad you made it," Nelson greeted him with a friendly smile.

"Yeah. Looking forward to the climb," he said, relaxing his cool-dude posture.

The rest of the group greeted each other with enthusiasm, their excitement infectious.

Wasting no time, Nelson asked, "Ready, gang?"

"Ready," they responded in unison, Frank's voice being the loudest.

Nelson and Oliver led, the girls followed, and Frank tailed as they began the trek, winding their way past slower hikers.

After the first quarter mile, Frank caught up to Jen, who trailed Cindy. When he tried to start a conversation, Jen shot him an annoyed look. She then accelerated her pace, echoing the group's training mantra of silence during training.

It was a grueling climb for Frank, who struggled to keep up. When they paused at the halfway point, he had to stop himself from guzzling down his entire water bottle. His muscles begged for relief, and his hot and swollen feet felt like they were cooking in his combat boots. Frank swore he was having a heart attack.

After splashing water on his face and neck, and resting for a few minutes, he calmed down and approached Cindy.

"Hey, you look worn out," she said, studying his face. "You okay?"

"Yeah," he coughed. "I'm fine."

"Are you sure?" she asked suspiciously.

"Yeah," he said, wiping sweat from his brow with the back of his hand.

She shrugged. "If you say so."

"So, tell me," asked Frank, "when did you all decide to start training together?"

"We've been hiking together since last summer."

"I wish I'd met you guys sooner. I've been doing this on my own for the last two months."

Cindy furrowed her brow, reminding Frank of his supposed appendectomy.

"I mean, before my surgery. So whose idea was it to start the …"

"All right gang," Nelson proclaimed, cutting off the remainder of Frank's question. "Let's get going."

Frank internally groaned.

"Mind if I walk with you, Cindy?"

"If you can keep up, sure."

Frank had nothing if not grit. For the next mile, he pushed himself to the limit, digging deep to keep up with Cindy's fast gait. But when he tried to chat with her, Cindy reminded him of Nelson's rule.

With labored breaths, Frank tried again. "I know we're not allowed to talk during training …" He breathed deeply and let it out slowly … "but can I drive you home so we can talk?"

Cindy hesitated to reply. She'd just met him after all, and although Frank came off nice, in her experience guys were usually out for one thing.

Frank waited, not certain if she'd heard him.

Cindy glanced at his boy scout-like, innocent face and decided he seemed trustworthy.

"Okay," she said, surprising Frank. "Provided you'll still be in shape to drive anywhere after this," she smiled.

"Oh, don't worry about me. I can do this in my sleep."

"Ha! Race you."

Increasing her pace, Cindy soon left him in the dust.

At Mount Minsi, the group replenished themselves with energy bars, grapes, and Gatorade. Grateful for the snacks shared, Frank kicked himself for not packing anything but two bottles of water. You'd think he'd learned after the first hike, but he still acted like an amateur, which, of course, he was.

Perspiring heavily, red-faced, and looking ready to lie down on the ground, the group eyed him with concern and more than a little annoyance.

After much hydration and stretching, they began their descent to the parking lot. Once there, the group high-fived one another for a successful hike. Frank, who to his credit, willed himself to finish the hike, celebrated along with them.

"Good job, Frank," said Nelson without conviction. The others nodded politely while busying themselves dumping their trash in the receptacles.

"Thanks," Frank said, knowing better.

"All right gang, let's get going," Nelson said, already walking toward his car.

"I'm riding with Frank," Cindy called out.

Nelson stopped. Everyone's attention fixed on him.

Without turning around, he said, "Okay, then, see you at school." He waved his hand and continued down to the parking lot.

That morning on the way to Lake Road to meet up with Frank, the group had agreed not to do their usual speed to give Frank grace for his recent surgery. Despite that, Frank struggled to keep up with this slower pace—a topic of conversation among the group on their way home.

"Damn, that was excruciating," Nelson remarked, a bit too pithily.

"Yeah," agreed Oliver. We could've finished earlier if it hadn't been for him."

"He tried talking to me, but I shut him down," Jen emphasized.

Nelson smirked, "Did you see his red and sweaty face?" The group burst into laughter.

By the time Nelson dropped off his first passenger, they had reached the consensus that they could not allow Frank to disrupt their routine, not when they vowed to be in shape for the Appalachian Trail in a few months. Nelson would later call Cindy to inform her of their decision to oust Frank. Although they were not dating, he couldn't help but feel jealous of the attention Cindy was giving to the newcomer. More importantly, Nelson was desperate to know what she and Frank had discussed during the half-hour drive to her house.

14

———————

*F*rank held open the car door for Cindy. Before stepping in, she asked, "Are you sure you're okay? You didn't look much like a hiker up there."

Frank hung his head and admitted, "Guess I'm not fully recovered."

"You better build your stamina gradually until you're strong enough to tackle a trail like Mount Minsi," she admonished.

"I'll try, but I don't think it's in my nature to slow down."

Cindy shook her head and got into the front passenger seat.

"So, where to, Cindy?" Frank asked, inserting the key into the ignition.

"I'm up 209 towards Marshalls Creek. I'll direct you as we get close."

Frank leisurely drove along, pausing at each intersection to give himself time to chat with Cindy.

"You did that hike like a pro," he said. I'm sure you'll be passing everyone soon."

"You think so?" she smiled broadly.

"A hundred percent."

"Nelson is the fastest one of our group though. If he were hiking alone, he would've done that trail in half the time."

"Maybe, but you're a runner-up for that title."

Although Cindy thought Frank was probably flirting, she did not feel apprehensive as she'd often felt with other boys. Something about him made it easy for her to let down her guard.

"Is Nelson your boyfriend?" asked Frank.

"What? No. We're just friends," she exclaimed. "What gave you that idea?"

"You may not have noticed, but Nelson has the hots for you."

She scoffed. "Believe me, I've noticed. I'm just not into him."

"It looked to me like you two had a beef."

"Not really. He kept asking me out. I turned him down nicely, but he wouldn't stop until I told him straight out that I would never go out with him."

"Ouch!"

"Yeah. I felt bad, but there was no other way to stop him."

"What about Jen and Oliver? Are they an item?"

"Hey, why do you want to know that?"

"They seem nice, that's all. Sorry."

Frank gave her a side-eyed look afraid he'd gone too far. She appeared pissed, her lips pursed.

"I'm sorry if I came across as nosy. Look, I don't have many friends … "

"I wonder why," she remarked.

Frank gave her a lopsided grin. "Okay, but like I said, I don't have many friends, and when I meet people I like, I want to know everything about them. Maybe that makes me weird, so I apologize."

Cindy turned to him. "You're likable. Don't try so hard to make friends." She pointed, "Turn right at the light."

Time was running out, and Frank had nothing. "Would you like to stop for a burger?" he blurted out.

The right-turn arrow flashed green, but Cindy had not responded.

Frank pushed the signal lever up and began to turn the wheel into the right lane.

"Yes," she finally replied.

Quickly straightening the car like a driver in unfamiliar territory, Frank provoked the long honk of the annoyed motorist who had to brake to avoid running into him.

"Whoa," cried Cindy, holding onto the door handle."

"Sorry about that," Frank said, turning off the right-turn indicator. "Where to?" he asked.

"How 'bout Muller's?" she suggested.

"Sure. I love that place."

After ordering their burgers with fries, a lemonade for Cindy and a Coke for Frank, Cindy said, "Jen and Oliver are friends, and that's all there is to it. She likes him, but he's more interested in books than dating."

"Nah, that only means he's not into Jen."

"Hmm. You may be right."

Frank took the plunge. "You think he was interested in Maceen?"

Cindy clicked her tongue. "Why are you so curious about her?"

Frank reached across the table and took her hand. She did not pull away.

"Even though I didn't know her, I can't seem to get her out of my mind."

Cindy noticed the genuine concern in his eyes, and even though she couldn't quite grasp why he cared, she was touched. "I think Oliver had puppy dog eyes for Maceen and had even asked her out a while back, but she told him she just wanted to be friends."

"Tell me about Maceen, Cindy. Were you close?"

"She's my best friend."

He gently squeezed her hand. "I'm sorry if I upset you."

She pulled her hand from his. "You didn't. I'm just frustrated that the police haven't found her."

Frank considered his next question.

"Sometimes it's the little things people say to the police that help solve a case."

"Like what?" she asked, furrowing her brow.

"Maybe there's a place, a neighbor, boyfriend, or someone else that a missing person might have mentioned before disappearing. Did Maceen ever mention anything like that to you?"

Before she could answer, the waitress placed their food on the table. "Will there be anything else," she asked.

"Cindy?" Frank asked.

"Oh no, this is fine."

Frank smiled at the waitress. "Thank you, but we're good for now."

"Let me know if you need anything else," she said, and walked away.

"Are you some kind of detective buff?" Cindy asked, squirting ketchup on her fries.

Frank coughed. "Who me? Nah, I like to solve mysteries. You might say I'm a detective wannabe." They both laughed.

"Look," Frank said, "I think people have secrets. Sometimes without meaning to, a clue to those secrets may slip out in conversation." He took a bite of his burger. "Oh, man, that's good."

Cindy sat straighter. "Wow, you're one of those deep thinkers, aren't you?"

Frank laughed out loud, almost choking on his burger. "I wouldn't say that."

Cindy took a bite of her burger and a sip of her lemonade, leaving Frank to wonder if she would answer the question.

"Maceen didn't have a boyfriend. She was serious about getting into college, and thought boys to be a distraction. The only guy she spent any time with is Oliver, but not in the way you think. They just studied together at the library."

"What makes you so sure they weren't involved? You said he had puppy dog eyes for her. Doesn't that mean he was into her?"

"Don't make me laugh," she giggled.

"What?"

"Take it from me. Maceen did not have any romantic interest in Oliver. They were just two brains preparing for college."

"Okay. I believe you."

Cindy twirled her straw in the icy lemonade, captivated by the swirling ice. Frank sensed she wanted to share more. He sipped his soda, giving her time to think.

Cindy stopped playing with her straw and declared, "Maceen told me that she met someone, and that they were planning to meet up at the library."

"Why the library?" he asked.

"She said her friend wanted to do some research, and since she was already going there to study, she offered to show him around."

"Him?"

"Yeah, but when I warned her to be careful since she'd just met him, she said that Oliver would also be at the library, so I had nothing to worry about. I had a feeling she was lying."

"About what?"

"That she would introduce him to Oliver before me," she said, taking a sip.

"Did she tell you his name or where he lived?"

"When I asked her, she changed the subject."

"Did you ask Oliver if Cindy brought him to the library the next time you saw him?"

Cindy sighed. "I meant to, but he was a bit late to training. Once he got there, we started the hike. I couldn't talk to him then because, as you know, we're not allowed to talk during training. And then, I completely forgot about it."

"That's understandable. You had a lot on your mind."

She let out a breath. "I suppose, but I wish I would've talked to Oliver about it." She again twirled her straw around the ice in her drink.

"Did you tell the police about your conversation with Maceen?"

She stopped playing with the straw and hissed, "Jesus, don't you ever stop?"

"I'm sorry, Cindy. I know it's hard."

Cindy crossed her arms and looked away, shutting herself off.

Afraid he'd pushed too hard, Frank gently said, "Never mind, Cindy. None of my business anyway." He picked up his burger.

After a moment, Cindy relaxed her arms, took a sip of lemonade, and said, "It never crossed my mind to mention Maceen's new friend to the police, okay? I was too upset when I heard she had gone missing. Besides, I didn't know who she was meeting, so what help would that have been to them?" She glared at him.

Frank acknowledged, "You're right. I'm sure the police questioned people at the library, including Oliver, so I wouldn't worry about it."

She sighed, sounding more relaxed. "I guess," she said.

"Did you ever get a chance to meet this mystery man?"

"When I asked her when she was going to bring him around, she said she would bring him to the next training. Oh shit!"

"What?"

"That was a week before she went missing." Cindy balled up her napkin and squeezed it tightly as tears filled her eyes.

Frank felt bad for pushing her so hard. "I'm sorry, Cindy. Please don't cry."

She suddenly pushed back her chair and without a word,

walked to the ladies' room where she had a good cry. When she returned, she faced Frank with red eyes, and said, "Look, I know you didn't mean to upset me, but you brought up a lot of painful memories for me."

"I'm sorry, Cindy."

She sat. "And I'm sorry for getting all emotional on you."

"You, emotional? Nah!"

She forced a weak smile.

"Hey, whatcha think of my hiking abilities?" asked Frank, going for a laugh.

She giggled. "Are you kidding? I thought you were going to have a heart attack, and that was an easy trail."

"I blame my appendectomy."

"Uh-huh."

"Eat your burger before it gets cold. Can I get you another drink?"

"Yes, please," replied Cindy, picking up her burger.

On their way home, Frank refrained from mentioning Maceen. He'd put Cindy through enough emotional turmoil and didn't want to alienate her. Instead, he asked, "Do you like to play video games?"

"Sure. I sometimes go to the arcade. I'm not very good, but I like to play. You?"

"Love them."

They spent the rest of the ride talking about video games.

When he dropped her off, Frank said, "Hey Cindy, thanks for hanging out with me today, and again, I'm sorry I upset you."

"That's okay. We're cool."

15

Monday, March 22, 2010

rank spent Saturday evening and all day Sunday recovering on the couch playing video games. While blowing up vehicles on screen, he wondered what questions to ask the hiking club when he met them again.

On Monday morning, he rose early, ready to engage in some rigorous weightlifting exercises. He had wasted too much time recovering and didn't want his muscles to weaken. He then indulged in a long and invigorating hot shower. Although he still hated hiking, he felt sufficiently rested to tackle Levee Loop, and looked forward to getting back to his undercover mission.

The weather forecast called for a cool start to the day, with periods of sun and clouds in the afternoon. After a hearty breakfast, he whistled while dressing in a t-shirt, sweatpants, and a zippered sweat shirt. He laced up his combat boots, and showed up for work on time.

"You look like you're ready for anything, Frank," Ruby snickered when he entered the agency.

"As Hamlet once said, Ruby, "The Readiness is All.""

"I take it Saturday's hike went well?"

"Let's just say I managed to finish the trail."

Unable to control herself, Ruby couldn't resist letting out a hearty guffaw. "You walked in here without limping, I'll give you that," she managed to say, wiping away tears of laughter.

"All right, all right. What's on the agenda this morning?" he asked.

Ruby picked up an envelope, still chuckling. "You can start by delivering this affidavit to the insurance company. I wrote the address on the envelope. Here's the pouch for the bank deposits. After that, check in on Mrs. Williamson's condition at Pocono Medical."

Frank grabbed the envelope and the pouch. "Boss in yet?"

"Not yet. You better get going if you want to leave early today. I'm sure he'll keep you busy until then."

"I hear that."

Upon his return to the office to inform Pierce about his conversation with Cindy, he discovered that Pierce had already come in and left again. Frank was determined not to be late for the hike. He assured Ruby that he would fill Pierce in after the hike and that he might have more information to share later.

Arriving at Dansbury Park on time, Frank waited for the group. As a few hikers walked by, he greeted them with a nod, feeling a sense of kinship. Checking his watch, he realized the kids were twenty minutes late. Regrettably, he hadn't asked Cindy for her phone number so he could check what was delaying them.

He was about to return to his car thinking the group had cancelled, when he spotted them coming up the path.

Nelson frowned when he saw Frank wave. The others bowed their heads.

What gives?

"Hey, gang," said Frank when they caught up to him. "Were you guys in detention?" He chuckled.

The group, including Cindy, avoided making eye contact.

Oh, oh, something's up.

"No, Frank, we weren't in detention," Nelson retorted sharply. "I changed the meeting time."

"Why'd you do that, Nelson?" he asked casually, though his stomach was doing somersaults.

"Here's the thing, Frank, we let you join our group because we thought you were a serious hiker."

Frank opened his mouth to protest, but Nelson raised his hand.

"And before you say it, I know you recently had surgery, but you slowed us down at Minsi man, and as you know, we don't have much time to prepare for the Appalachian Trail. So we think you should find another group to train with. No offense."

"Was this a unanimous decision?" Frank asked, glancing around, hoping someone would defend him. The group fidgeted as if on cue, and remained silent.

"Yes. Sorry, Frank. It's for the best. Nothing against you, but we can't jeopardize our progress. You understand."

Frank turned to Cindy. "You feel that way too, Cindy?"

"I do. You're not ready, Frank" she said, lowering her gaze.

"Okay. Good luck then. It was nice meeting you all."

"Yeah, bye, Frank," said Nelson. "Let's go, guys. We've wasted enough time." The team obediently followed, keeping their eyes on Nelson. Cindy mouthed, "Sorry," as she passed by Frank.

He watched them until they were out of sight.

Frank thought he had better call the boss.

After filling up at a Marshalls Creek gas station, Pierce pondered his next move.

About to drive away, his cell phone rang.

"Pierce."

"Boss, they kicked me out," Frank lamented.

"Who kicked you out, Frank?" Pierce asked, knowing the answer.

"The hiking group. Nelson, their bossy leader, convinced them I was slowing them down."

Pierce shook his head, trying not to laugh. "Well, they are serious hikers, Frank. Don't take it personally."

"I know, but it stings a bit."

Pierce smiled and asked, "Did you at least get some useful information?"

"You bet."

"Let's hear it."

"After the hike on Saturday, I took Cindy for a burger, and we had a long conversation about Maceen and the other members of the group. I got carried away with the questions and made her cry, but in the end, I think she forgave me."

"Oh no, Frank. Did you at least get anything useful from her?"

"I did. Maceen shared a secret with Cindy a week before she vanished. Said she was going to ditch work to meet up with a guy at the library to do some research. She reassured Cindy that Oliver would be there too."

"Hmm."

"Maceen didn't disclose how she met him or anything else about the guy. All she would say is that she would bring him around to meet the hiking team. Cindy suspected that Maceen was lying because as her best friend, she felt Maceen would have introduced him to her before anyone else. She meant to confirm with Oliver if Maceen had indeed come to the library with her new friend, but when she again saw him at practice, she didn't get the chance and later forgot about it."

"I suppose Maceen didn't mention the name of this new friend."

"Nope," but I got the feeling Cindy was holding something back."

"Why's that?"

"Just a feeling. Don't best friends tell each other everything? How come Cindy didn't know more about this mysterious fellow? Could it be she didn't have all the details, or that she didn't want to betray her friend by telling me?"

"Good point."

"If we are to believe Cindy that Maceen was evasive with what little she revealed, it may be that Maceen believed that if she introduced her new friend to the group, she'd be met with disapproval."

"Because?" prompted Pierce.

"Maybe he's older or a high school dropout. Perhaps he's a recovering addict, or something else which may cause her embarrassment in front of her friends. Who knows what a teenager will hide from her peers, let alone her parents?"

"Makes sense. Anything else?"

"I asked if Jen and Oliver were an item, but Cindy laughed. She said Oliver had puppy dog eyes for Maceen."

"That's something to think about."

"I'll say. Oliver was into Maceen, but according to Cindy, Maceen never noticed. At that point, Cindy was getting upset with my reminding her of Maceen, so I had to change the subject. If they hadn't kicked me out of the group, I'm sure I would have learned more."

"I appreciate you stepping up and trying something your body was not used to doing, and you got information we didn't have. So cheer up. You hate hiking anyway."

"Yes, it's torture. I hate it so much," Frank laughed.

"I do have another job for you, though."

"Great. What do you want me to do? Climb Mt. Everest? Cause I'll do it."

"Ha, ha. No, nothing physical. I would like you to see if you could interview one or two of the team members, especially Oliver, now that we know how he felt about Maceen."

Frank groaned. "I'll talk to Oliver, but I'm persona non grata with that group. I don't think the others will want to talk to me, especially Nelson."

"You'll find a way, Frank."

He inhaled, "I'll do my best."

"That's the spirit, and since you've established a rapport with Cindy, you can try to talk to her again. See if she has anything else to share."

"Good idea. Gives me a chance to further dig into what she knows about Maceen's movements before she vanished. I'll drop by her neighborhood later this evening and see if I can catch up with her."

"All right. I'm on my way to check out a possible lead."

"Okay, goodbye, boss."

"Bye, Frank."

16

*P*ierce arrived at Bon-ton's and promptly asked a cashier for the manager. To avoid calling his boss, the cashier politely inquired, "May I be of assistance?"

"Thank you, no. I need to speak to the manager."

Reluctantly, the cashier dialed an extension and whispered, "There's a gentleman here requesting to speak to the manager … I tried … he wants to talk to you … looks like a cop … okay." He hung up and turned to Pierce. "She'll be with you in a moment."

"Thank you."

While he waited, Pierce decided to question the cashier. "How long have you worked here?"

"Three years now," he replied, folding returned garments.

"Full time?"

"Yes, all week and sometimes on Saturdays."

"I suppose weekends are busiest?"

The cashier grabbed another garment and looked around. "Oh yeah. As you can see, not many people shop during the week."

"Do you remember Maceen Robinson? She used to work here part time."

"Well, sure. She was all over the news when she disappeared."

"Ever talk to her?"

By this point, the cashier was convinced he was speaking to a policeman. He paused his folding, envisioning media fame for assisting the police in finding the missing girl, even though he barely knew Maceen. "The police questioned everyone when it happened," he said knowingly. "Is there any new information?"

"I can't talk about that."

"Oh, no. Of course not."

"Talk to Maceen?" Pierce reminded him.

The cashier leaned forward conspiratorially. "We weren't what you call friends, but she was pleasant enough. She asked me a few questions when she first started working here, but once she learned the ropes, she'd just say hi and bye to me. You know how teens are, they don't like talking to us old folks." He let out a hearty laugh, but it quickly faded when he looked past Pierce—All thoughts of fame vanishing. "Here comes the manager," he said, turning away to fold garments once more.

A woman who appeared to be in her forties, with a friendly but professional demeanor, strode to the cashiers' station.

"Hello, I'm Shirley Givens, the manager. You wanted to speak with me?"

"Yes, Miss Givens." He glanced at the cashier who was all ears. "Is there somewhere we can speak in private?"

"Yes, follow me."

In her office she pulled up a chair for Pierce and sat at her desk. "What's this about?"

"I understand Maceen Robinson worked part time at this store."

Although convinced Pierce was the police, she sought to

verify this information before determining which employee details she was permitted to disclose.

"Are you a police officer?"

"Former homicide detective, now private investigator." He pulled out his card and extended it to her.

Givens studied the card and returned it.

Before she asked, Pierce said, "I've been hired by Maceen's parents to investigate their daughters' disappearance since attention to the case has diminished."

"You understand I can't give you any personal information without a warrant," she said.

"Certainly, ma'am. I have but a few questions for you."

"All right. I'll decide if I can answer them. Go ahead, ask your questions."

"How long did Maceen work here?"

"Not long. A few months, actually. She called to quit the day before news broke that she was missing."

"Give a reason?"

"I asked why she was quitting a job she apparently enjoyed doing, but she abruptly hung up. The previous weekend, she had called in sick." Givens shook her head. "I was deeply saddened to learn of her disappearance on the news."

"Did you ever notice a customer seek her out?"

"Maceen was friendly, and yes, one or two of our customers sought her out for advice, but what you're asking is if anyone suspicious approached her?"

"I am."

She picked up a pen and began to tap it on her desk. "Hiring teenagers comes with a unique set of challenges. Some lack initiative and need encouragement to step up and contribute more actively, some call off work with little notice, or they simply come here and goof off, doing the bare minimum. Maceen was a model employee. She seemed to enjoy helping our customers. I'm not usually on the floor unless there's an issue or I'm making my rounds, but other than boys her age trying to flirt, I never witnessed a customer speak to her in a manner that I would consider inappropriate or suspicious."

"What about friends? Ever see her with them?"

"Hmm. Let me think. I did see one particular boy pick her up after her shift a couple of times. I assumed he was a friend."

"Can you describe him?"

"Tall, thin with a nice smile."

"Anything else about him you recall?"

"He wore his hair in an afro."

"All right. Thank you for seeing me, Miss Givens."

"I'm sorry I couldn't be of more help."

"Not at all. Every piece of information, no matter how insignificant it may seen, helps me get closer to solving her disappearance. Thank you for seeing me."

Pierce, who had intended to visit the library since he was in the neighborhood, was disappointed to learn that it was closed for the day.

17

*a*fter being expelled from the hiking club, Frank found himself wondering if Cindy would speak to him again. He guessed that she would be home after the group's usual hike late that afternoon. Determined to reconnect, Frank decided to drive by her house and see if she would talk to him. But once he got there, he worried she might think he was interested in her romantically by showing up unannounced.

What was I thinking?

As he began to pull out of her driveway, he heard a familiar voice call out to him.

Frank checked his rearview mirror and saw Cindy walking toward him.

He shifted the car into Park and rolled down his window.

As she approached, she asked, "What are you doing here, Frank?"

Frank, once again, had to think quickly. "I'm picking up a pizza from Petrizzo's for my mom. Since I'm in the area, I figured I'd swing by to see if you'd like to hang out with me while I wait."

"But you changed your mind?"

"Huh?"

"You were backing out of my driveway."

Frank hung his head, acting contrite. "Yeah, I chickened out."

Cindy smiled. "I have a book report to write, but I'll wait with you."

"Cool, hop in." Frank leaned over to unlock the door. "How was the hike?" he asked as she buckled up.

"Oh, you know," she shrugged, looking straight ahead. "The usual."

To put her at ease, Frank lied, "Guess what? I've already teamed up with a friend who hikes every day. He's not interested in tackling the Appalachian Trail, says he hikes for fun, but I'm pretty sure he'll get me ready."

Cindy perked up. "That's wonderful, Frank. Maybe you can join us when you feel stronger. Just don't push yourself too hard until you're fully healed," she admonished, giving him a playful nudge.

"I won't."

Frank pulled into the parking lot at Petrizzo's and noticed a few people in line waiting to place their orders. He said, "This might be a while. Would you like a slice and a drink while we wait?

"Sure, I'll have a slice, and a lemonade, please."

"Anything on your pizza?"

"No thanks. I like mine plain."

"Plain it is." He looked around, noticed an empty table, and pointed. "Why don't you go grab that table over there while I order?"

"Okay."

Frank soon walked over carrying a tray with two slices, a lemonade for her, and a Coke for him. He set the tray in the center of the table and pulled out a couple of napkins from the holder. "Oops," he said, "I forgot the straws. Be right back."

"He quickly got back and handing her a straw, said, "They'll let me know when my order's ready." He sat opposite her and picked up his slice, blowing on it before taking a cautious bite.

"Cindy," he began, as she also blew on her slice of pizza and took a bite, "remember when I told you I'm a detective wannabe?"

"Yeah?" she asked, her expression turning serious.

"I was wondering if you knew of any place Maceen may have gone to when she left home?"

Cindy dropped her slice on the paper plate.

"Oh my God! Do you actually believe she ran away from home and that I know where she is?"

Fuck me!

"No, no, that's not what I meant," he said.

"Don't you believe I want to know what happened to my best friend?" she exclaimed, frustrated with his probing questions. "I'm beginning to think you're asking me all these questions about her just to satisfy your morbid curiosity."

Frank reached across the table and lightly touched her hand. She recoiled.

Shit!

"No, no, Cindy. It's not that. Look, I know you cared for her, but it's like I told you, it's the little things someone says that may lead to a clue in solving a case."

"And what exactly are you going to do with what I've already shared with you?"

Frank thought he'd better give her a reasonable explanation. "Perhaps I can convince the private detective my mom works for to look into it."

Cindy's eyes widened. "Your mom works for a private detective?"

"Yeah. Maybe he can help."

Cindy thought for a moment. "So that's why all the questions." She grabbed her drink, emptied the cup, and contemplated this new information. "Do you think a private detective will find her, even though the police are clueless?"

Frank shrugged. "Maybe."

Cindy lowered her head, thinking it over. "You've made me think of things I didn't want to face, Frank."

Frank swallowed. "I'm so stupid. Of course, you don't want to talk about it. I'm sorry for bringing it up again."

"Why didn't you tell me about the private detective until now? If you'd been truthful, I would've understood."

"Honestly, I didn't think you'd believe me. I've been following this case since she disappeared—I felt bad, and wanted to help. That part is true."

An uncomfortable silence hung in the air between them, neither making eye contact.

Finally, Cindy said, "Okay, I'll answer a few more questions. After this, I don't ever want you to ask me about Maceen again." She blew out a breath. "What else do you want to know that you haven't already asked me?"

Frank hesitated for a moment.

"Ask your questions," she demanded, raising her voice.

"All right. You said Maceen spent her free time studying, but didn't the boys at school ask her out?"

"Yes, of course, but she turned them all down."

Frank nodded. "Are you certain you didn't notice any changes in her behavior around the time she disappeared that made you suspect she was seeing someone?

Cindy bit her lip.

Frank sensed she was hiding something.

"Cindy?" pushed Frank.

She sniffled. "The last time I saw Maceen was the Thursday before she disappeared. She mentioned she was thinking about quitting her job. I found it strange, since she loved working at the store."

"Where was she working?"

"She and I work part-time at Bon-Ton's in the mall."

"Oh wow, my mom loves that store," he said, hoping to put her at ease.

"So does mine."

"Do you both work in the same department?"

"No. She works in Men's Clothing. I work in Cosmetics."

"Do the other members of the hiking club work at the mall too?" He smiled encouragingly.

"Jen and Nelson work at the concession stand at the movie theatre. Oliver doesn't have a job."

"He studies," they both said simultaneously, easing the tension between them.

"They ever give you free snacks?"

"I wish. Seriously though, Jen and Nelson like their jobs and wouldn't do anything to get them fired, and you know Nelson, he's a stickler for the rules."

"Yeah, learned that from experience."

Now that Cindy was in a lighter mood, Frank chanced another question.

"Did you ask Maceen why she was thinking about quitting a job she loved?"

Cindy sighed and she sank into her seat, their shared moment of glee over. "I did ask her, but I guess she saw the look on my face and said she was kidding."

"Did you believe her?"

"I don't know. Maceen liked to fool around sometimes."

"Want another lemonade?" asked Frank.

"Yes, please."

Frank was about to rise when the waitress came over with their order.

"Thank you."

He could have asked the waitress to bring Cindy another drink but he wanted to give her time to think things through.

93

"I'll get your lemonade and pay for my order. Eat your pizza before it gets cold."

She hadn't touched her pizza when he returned, but gratefully accepted the lemonade and took a big swig.

"Do you remember anything else Maceen may have said or done before she disappeared?"

Cindy blew out an exasperated breath and took another sip. She said, "This might not be important, but a few weeks before Maceen told me about her new friend, she dragged me to the bookstore at the mall to buy a book on botany. Maceen was set to go to Penn State for environmental studies, hoping to one day work for the EPA, so I didn't get why she would buy such a book."

"Perhaps botany ties in with the study of environmental science."

"Oh. I never thought of that."

"Did you ask her why she bought that book?"

"No. She never gave me the chance. After paying for it, she began to talk about a top she wanted to buy at Sears and dragged me out of the bookstore. We spent the next hour shopping, and I forgot about the book. Do you think her buying that particular book is important?"

"I wouldn't worry about it. I mean, how can a book help the police find Maceen? If it were that easy, they would've solved the case by now."

"Yeah, that makes sense," she agreed, and finished her drink.

Frank gathered their paper plates of cold, uneaten pizza, napkins and cups and dumped them in the garbage before picking up his 'mom's pizza.'

Cindy remained silent during the short ride home. Once they reached her driveway, Frank asked, "Are you okay?"

"I know you mean well, Frank, but you have no idea how scared I was when Maceen disappeared. I called and texted her every day for a month. After a while, I had to stop trying to contact her. I was barely sleeping or eating. I meant what I said earlier. I don't ever want you to ask me about her again. Your questions make me feel guilty."

"What about?"

With a trembling voice, she groused, "About not telling the police that I suspected my friend had lied to me." She sniffled. "What proof did I have for them, anyway?"

"I didn't mean to make you feel guilty about any of that, Cindy. I'm sorry."

"Goodnight, Frank." Cindy opened the car door, stepped out, and slammed it shut without looking back. Frank thought about calling Pierce, but looking at his watch, he decided to wait until he got into the office in the morning.

18

Tuesday, March 23, 2010

*A*t the library, several students were engrossed in their reading and note-taking, conversing quietly amongst themselves. Pierce noticed Oliver sitting alone, with several books open on the table. He held one book in his hand, deeply concentrating on its contents.

A woman, seated a few feet away from the students, who appeared to be in her late sixties, caught his attention. Her shoulder-length brown hair was braided in a long braid, streaked with red highlights.

Pierce watched as she paused her reading to stare in the direction of the teenagers. Someone caught her eye, prompting her to close her book and retrieve a sketchbook and pencil from her tote bag. After fifteen minutes of drawing, she closed her pad, put it and her pencil back in her bag, and prepared to depart.

Pierce walked over and introduced himself. "Hello, I'm a private investigator working on a case involving the disappearance of Maceen Robinson. Can we chat?"

"Oh, I remember that name," she said, peering at Pierce through her stylish and colorful blue and red glasses.

"Would you mind if I ask you a few questions?"

Intrigued, she set down her bag. "Pull up a chair."

Pierce grabbed a chair from the nearby table and positioned it across from her.

As soon as he sat down, she started chatting. "I saw you observing the kids studying over there." She tilted her head towards the students. "Clearly, you don't come here to read, leading me to presume that you are either telling me the truth that you are a private investigator, or a pervert," she declared without humor. "Have ID on you?"

"Yes, ma'am." Pierce reached into his pocket, pulled out his card, and offered it to her.

After a moment's consideration, she returned his identification without commenting on his former occupation as a homicide detective.

"Okay, Mr. Pierce, what is it you want to know? And please, call me Wendy. That ma'am title makes me feel like an old lady," she snickered.

His cell phone buzzed in his pocket but Pierce ignored it.

"Gonna get that?"

"It can wait."

"If you say so."

"Do you come here often, Wendy?"

"Not every day but often enough. Been coming here for the past three years since my husband passed. Fills the days."

"Sorry for your loss."

"No need. He was a bit of a dick," she sighed wistfully, "but still … I do miss him."

He gave her a half-hearted smile wondering if she was kidding, and pulled out a photo of Maceen from his notebook. He reached across the table to show her. "Do you recognize her?"

She glanced at the photo briefly and nodded, "Yes, of course. That's Maceen Robinson. The police questioned me after her disappearance." She gave the photo back to Pierce.

"Why did the police question you?" he asked, tucking the photo back into his notebook.

"Same reason you're doing so now. I'm here most days of the week. They wanted to know if I'd seen any strange people around Maceen."

"And did you?"

"No. That girl came here to study." She turned her head and gestured with her chin. "With that boy over there sitting by himself, with his head in the book."

When Pierce identified Oliver earlier, he made the decision that engaging in conversation with him would not result in a better outcome than if Frank were to approach the youth.

"Is there something you later remembered that you didn't mention to the police?" asked Pierce.

Wendy thought for a moment and said, "The week she went missing, I heard the kids whisper that the cops were all over them at school, so I don't understand what you think you'll find out that the police haven't."

"Perhaps nothing, but I need to be able to go back to the parents with either a lead, or to say I've failed to find their daughter, and I'd rather it not be the latter."

Wendy nodded.

"If you don't mind me asking? Are you an artist?" Pierce inquired.

She smiled. "Not an artist in a professional sense but I like to sketch people for fun."

Pierce's internal antennae vibrated. "Mind if I take a peek?"

"I sense the reason you ask is to see if I have a sketch of a person of interest. Correct?"

"You may have sketched someone responsible for Maceen's disappearance without realizing it."

"Of course, but that would have been months ago," she said flicking her long braid back.

"Any chance you kept those drawings?"

"Like I said, I do this for fun, so no, I don't keep them for more than a day."

She saw the disappointment in Pierce's eyes. "Ah, I see," she nodded. "You were hoping to have a look at my old sketches."

"They may have revealed someone worth talking to."

"Bit of a stretch, don't you think?"

He shrugged. "You never know, Wendy."

She pinched her lips trying to decide if she should share her sketchbook with the inquisitive detective. Ultimately, she retrieved it and pushed it toward Pierce.

Pierce grabbed the notebook and slowly turned the pages. Her latest sketch was of a girl sitting two tables away with a pensive look on her face trying to work out a problem. The other sketches were mostly of students diligently studying or engaged in hushed conversations among themselves. Some sketches also showed parents helping their children pick out a book from the shelves. Pierce closed the book.

"These are very good. You should do this professionally."

"That ship has sailed, but thank you for the compliment."

She reached for her sketchbook. "I hope you break the case and that girl is found. I hate to think what her parents are going through." She packed up her tote and left.

Pierce had one more stop to make before heading back to the office.

19

rank had spent the entire day in and out of the office without ever seeing Pierce, who had been following up on the interviews. Eager to discuss his conversation with Cindy, Frank decided to catch up with Pierce at the library after he had spoken to Ruby, who informed him that Pierce would be there. He also hoped to find Oliver, whom he believed would be more receptive to talking away from Nelson's influence. After his ouster from the group and his talk with Cindy, Frank wasn't up to facing the rest of the team.

Pulling into the parking lot, he spotted Pierce about to drive away. Frank honked and waved, catching Pierce's attention.

Pierce turned off the engine and waited patiently for Frank to pull up next to him.

"Hi, boss," Frank said, getting into the front passenger seat. "I have some news."

Pierce lowered the volume on the radio and turned to Frank. "I'm listening."

"A few weeks before Maceen vanished, she was at the mall with Cindy when Maceen insisted on going to the book store. She bought a book on botany, which surprised Cindy since

Maceen had never shown an interest in plants, despite her plans to study environmental science in college. I told Cindy botany may be part of that study. But what do I know, right?" he chortled. "Maceen didn't explain to Cindy why she bought that book and rushed her out of the store as soon as she paid for it. By the way, Jen and Nelson work at the mall, in the concession stand of the movie theatre. Cindy works in the Cosmetics Department, while Maceen worked in Men's Clothing, both at Bon-Tons."

"Yes. I spoke with Maceen's boss," said Pierce. "She confirmed Maceen called in sick the weekend prior to her disappearance, and again on the Thursday before to quit her job without giving any explanation."

"Cindy said Maceen told her she was thinking about quitting her job, but when Cindy asked her why she would quit a job she loved, Maceen said she was kidding. Looks to me like Maceen quit her job to run away with her boyfriend," Frank said.

"We can't rule that out, Frank, but there might be another explanation. We'll need to investigate further before coming to any conclusions."

"Yes, boss."

"When I visited the Robinsons, I saw that botany book on Maceen's desk in her bedroom. Thanks for helping me fill in a piece of the puzzle, Frank."

"You figured out why she bought that book?"

"I'm working on it."

"Okay then. I was just about to go inside to see Oliver. I hope I didn't miss him."

"He's still there."

"Cool."

"Let me know how it goes."

"Will do."

As he drove away, Pierce thought about the botany book and the unidentified plant in Maceen's bedroom.

He looked at his watch, turned up the volume to "Twist & Shout" playing on the radio, and headed back to the office.

———

FRANK WAS ABOUT to enter the library, when Oliver, book bag slung over his shoulder, emerged from the automatic doors. He blinked at the bright sunlight and pulled out his sunglasses from his pocket.

"Hi Oliver," Frank said, accosting him. "How's it going?"

Oliver nearly dropped his shades and backed away. Awkwardly trying to fit them on, he uttered, "Okay."

"Hiking going well?"

Oliver grimaced. "I really must be going, Frank." He hastened away eager to get away from this person he barely knew.

"Why the hurry? It's not as if you have a job to go to."

Oliver stopped. "What do you want, Frank?"

"Just a friendly chat."

Oliver took in a deep breath, trying to keep his cool. "What is it" he asked impatiently."

Frank made a quick decision. "I'm gonna be honest with you, Oliver." He lowered his voice. "I work for a private detective hired by Maceen's parents."

Oliver laughed. "What? You mean you were pretending to be a hiker? That explains why you're miserable at it." He proceeded toward his car, believing Frank was playing a joke on him.

Frank walked along with him. "Yeah, hiking's not for me, but seriously, Oliver, do you have a minute so we can talk?"

"Leave me alone, Frank. I don't know why you're lying about working for a PI, but I'm not gonna play your game."

Frank grabbed his arm. "It's not a game, and I'm not a teenager, Oliver. Take off the shades and look closely at my face."

Oliver slowly removed his sunglasses and stared, unsure of what he was supposed to see. Confused, he conceded that Frank could be older.

"I work for the Bloodhound Detective Agency. We're investigating Maceen's disappearance." Frank glanced around. "It's too crowded here for us to have a proper conversation. Why don't you let me buy you a cold drink. Whaddya say?"

"I'm not going anywhere with you," Oliver replied, nervously.

"C'mon, man. I know you want to help find Maceen," Frank insisted.

Oliver contemplating his next move, clicked his tongue. "Okay, okay," he said, his curiosity getting the better of him.

"Follow me to the mall," Frank said.

At the food court, cold drinks in front of them, Frank began his interrogation.

"Did you know Maceen was going to ditch work on the weekend she disappeared?"

Oliver flinched. "Why would I know that?"

"Cause you two were friends."

"That doesn't mean she confided in me," he said, in a squeaky voice.

"Seriously, Oliver, did you know of Maceen's plans to ditch work?"

Oliver looked everywhere but at Frank, undecided about what to reveal.

"Oliver?"

"Yeah, all right? She told me she didn't like to work at the mall and was going to quit."

Frank thought for a moment. "Was she seeing someone?"

"Seeing someone?"

"You know what I mean. Did she act like she dug somebody?"

Oliver averted his eyes. "I don't know, man."

"Think hard, Oliver. This is important."

He exhaled forcefully. "She may have mentioned meeting a guy, but that doesn't mean she dug him," he insisted.

Hit a nerve?

"This guy got a name?"

Oliver focused on the melting ice in his cup, deliberately avoiding Frank's gaze.

"Do you know his name?" Frank asked again.

"She never said," Oliver mumbled, his eyes fixed on his soda.

Frank decided to rattle him. "How did you feel being so close to a girl you were secretly in love with?"

Caught off guard, Oliver shrunk into his seat.

He stammered, "She was my ... study buddy ... that's all."

"Sure, pal." Frank took a sip of his ginger ale, watching Oliver closely. "Did Maceen know how you felt about her?"

"What has that got to do with anything?" He stared daggers at Frank, grabbed his drink with a shaky hand, and gulped it down.

Frank waited. When Oliver put down the cup, Frank pronounced, "What it has to do with, Oliver, is that it makes you a suspect in her disappearance, that's what."

"I'm not responsible for what happened," he coughed, raising his voice and drawing attention.

"Keep your voice down," Frank warned. "Did you tell the police how you felt about her?"

He shook his head, forcefully. "They had no reason to know that."

Frank scoffed. "Yeah, Oliver. They most certainly needed to know that, but we'll move on. "Are you sure you're not aware of your competition's name?" he teased.

Oliver sighed. "You got it all wrong. Maceen wasn't into me. We were just friends."

"I hear you, but you were close, close enough to share secrets, I bet."

"We weren't the kind of friends who told each other everything. Talk to Cindy. She was Maceen's best friend."

Frank grew tired of the cat and mouse game. He warned Oliver, "You're not leaving here until you tell me the name of that guy she wanted you to meet."

Oliver went pale. He clenched his jaw, and through gritted teeth, hissed, "Damn you, Frank. I said, *I ... don't ... know.*"

"Frank leaned in, almost touching Oliver's face. He whispered, "I think you do know."

He leaned back, and in a friendly tone, said, "Take your time. Want another soda? Something to eat?"

Oliver, who looked like a trapped animal, nervously replied, "No. What I truly want is for you to leave me alone."

"Sure, buddy, as soon as we're done here."

If looks could kill, Frank would've swooned on the spot.

A few minutes of silence went by. Frank emptied his cup and began chewing on the ice. Oliver sat with his head down, wondering what to do.

At last, he blurted, "I think Maceen said his name was ... Zack ... or Jack?" He shook his head. "No that's not it."

"C'mon, Oliver, think."

"Matt," he blurted. "Yeah, Matt."

"Matt have a last name?"

"Just Matt."

"Okay. One more thing. Did Maceen get along with her parents?"

"What kind of question is that?"

"Did Maceen get along with her parents?" Frank repeated.

"Yes, all right? She got along with them. They're nice

people." Exasperated with all the questions, Oliver said, "I really should be going now."

Frank thought for a moment and decided he wasn't going to get more out of Oliver. He pushed back his chair. "Thanks, buddy. I appreciate the info."

Oliver couldn't get out of the mall fast enough, colliding with the nearby table as he shot out of his seat.

"One more thing," Frank warned, following him out of the food court, "Please do not discuss our conversation with anyone. That includes friends or family. I wouldn't want to tip off anyone connected to the case."

"Don't worry about it. I won't tell a soul, he said, quickening his step."

In his car, Oliver let out his pent-up energy and started crying. He had convinced himself that Maceen was gone from his life. But then, Frank comes along claiming to be working for a private detective, and forced him to think about that terrible day.

20

_____

The last time Maceen and Oliver went hiking with the team, she surprised him when she caught up to him on the trail. Without facing him, she whispered, "Oliver, can you meet me at the Sears parking lot tonight, around eight?" Oliver turned to face her, his heart pounding in his chest.

"Don't look at me," she admonished. "We don't want to get in trouble for talking."

He faced forward, and imagined her yearning to take their friendship to the next level. In a fleeting moment, he envisioned them holding hands at the movie theatre, chatting on the phone till all hours of the night, and holding her close in an embrace.

"Well? Can you meet me or not?" she asked, shattering his fantasy.

"Yes," he replied, giddy with happiness.

She gushed, "I have something to tell you, but you first have to promise to keep it a secret."

Oliver was taken aback by the closeness of their conversation, yet he was also thrilled, and intrigued.

"What is it?" he asked, feeling special that she would trust him with a secret.

"Promise first," she insisted.

"I promise," he vowed, his heart racing with a mix of hope and trepidation. He yearned for her to reciprocate his feelings and show him that she cared for him more than just a friend.

"I think I'm in love with someone," she said.

And with that, Oliver's bubble burst, and he realized she'd never feel the same way about him as he did about her.

Accustomed to hiding his feelings, Oliver forced a smile. "Wow. Who?"

Jen looked behind her and shouted, "Hey you two. Catch up."

"Be right there," Maceen called back.

"We better increase our pace," Oliver suggested.

Maceen grabbed his arm and slowed them down. "You don't know him, and you're the only one I've told."

"Not even Cindy?" he asked, trying to ignore her fingers wrapped around his arm.

"No. She would be the first to object."

"Why?"

"He's a few years older than I am."

Oliver shrank away, surprised. "Shit, Maceen. Are you sure about this guy?"

"I've never been more sure. I'll introduce him to the team soon, but I wanted you to meet him first."

"Me? Why?"

"I just want you to meet him before the others, okay?"

What Maceen failed to perceive when she confided in Oliver, was his concealed anguish. Selfishly, she felt unburdened sharing her secret with him.

Seeking to escape her, Oliver said, "We better catch up." He sprinted as fast as he could, leaving her behind. At the end of the trail, he hastily announced he had something urgent to do, and dashed off.

After a shower and a change of clothes, Oliver tried to take his mind off Maceen by playing a computer chess game. After losing three games in a row, he turned off the computer, tears clouding his eyes, trying to decide if it would be a good idea to torture himself by meeting Maceen's new boyfriend.

At the dinner table, Oliver's family, oblivious to his turmoil, engaged in conversation with him while he maintained his customary amiable demeanor and prattled on about his schoolwork, the hike, and the upcoming Thanksgiving Day holiday. Throughout the meal, he pondered whether to meet up with Maceen. In the end, he had to meet the guy who stole Maceen's heart.

After dinner, he announced, "I'm gonna go over to Nelson's for a little while to check out his new video game." The library had closed, and although he'd never played video games with Nelson, he couldn't think of an excuse to leave the house. He detested lying to his parents, but couldn't tell them he was on his way to meet Maceen's boyfriend. He could hardly believe it himself.

Oliver's father raised an eyebrow because once Oliver came home from the library, he was in for the night. Ultimately, he said, "Be home by ten. It's a school night."

"I will," he promised.

When he parked at Sears, Oliver spotted Maceen talking animately with someone, whom he assumed to be *him*. He took a few deep breaths to calm his racing heart and to suppress his jealous feelings. After a few minutes, he turned off the ignition and donned his customary, friendly face. He then casually walked over to the couple.

"Hi, you must be Matt," greeted Oliver as he interrupted their conversation."

"Yes. Nice to meet you," said Matt, with a friendly smile.

"Hi, Oliver," Maceen said.

"Maceen's told me a lot about you," said Matt.

Oliver nearly gasped when he notice Matt was more than a

couple of years older than Maceen. He appeared to be in his mid-twenties. Oliver forced himself not to react and managed to say, "All good things, I hope."

"For sure."

"How'd you guys meet?" Oliver couldn't help asking, looking directly at Matt.

But it was Maceen who answered. "His father lives in my neighborhood."

"Oh, so you've known each other for a while," Oliver commented, not taking his eyes off Matt.

Matt wrapped his arm around Maceen's shoulders, and Oliver interpreted it as a message that Maceen is his girlfriend. He replied, "I've been away at school, so we hadn't met until this summer, but that's long enough to know that we like one another." He winked at Maceen, who was staring up at him. She smiled back.

Oliver inwardly winced—Message received. He asked, "Where are you guys off to? The mall's closed."

"Gonna get some pizza. Wanna come?" Maceen invited.

"Nah. Already ate, but you guys enjoy. I gotta go finish a homework assignment. Just wanted to stop by to meet you, Matt."

"Take care, man. It was nice to meet you too," said Matt.

"Yeah. Bye, Maceen."

"See you tomorrow," Maceen said, as Oliver hurried away, wondering if somehow he could convince her to stop seeing this handsome, charming, older man. His face dropped, remembering the look on Maceen's face when Matt put his arm around her.

After meeting him, Oliver couldn't resist the urge to fantasize about a plan to split them apart. *For her own good*, he thought.

But he never got the chance. At their last study session

before Maceen disappeared, she asked Oliver, "What did you think of Matt? Isn't he great?"

"He seems like a nice person, Maceen, but don't you think he's too old for you?" Oliver asked.

Maceen's face turned red with anger. "I didn't tell the others about him because I knew they wouldn't approve. I thought you, at least, would want me to be happy."

"I'm glad you're happy, but I'm worried about you," Oliver replied.

"Don't worry, he would never hurt me," was the last thing she said to him, before storming out of the library.

21

*P*ierce was about to walk away, after knocking three times, when the door swung open. A burly man in his sixties, standing at six feet three inches tall and dressed in a plaid shirt, jeans and slippers, opened the door with an expression of annoyance. "May I help you?" he asked in a subtle German accent.

"Mr. Josef Schmidt?"

"Yes," he replied cautiously.

"My name is Howard Pierce. I'm a private detective investigating the disappearance of Miss Maceen Robinson."

"What?" he scoffed, "The police were here months ago asking about that girl."

"Yes, sir, but despite their efforts to locate her, she's still missing. I have been entrusted by her parents with the responsibility of delving deeper into her disappearance."

With a look of consternation, Schmidt stated, "I don't see how I can add anything to what I've already told the police. Wait a minute," he stepped back, "do you think I had anything to do with that?"

Afraid he would slam the door in his face, Pierce assured

him, "Oh no, sir. I'm speaking with everyone previously interviewed by the police to ensure the parents are satisfied. It will only take a few minutes."

Schmidt hesitated for a moment before stepping aside. "Come in."

In the living room, a small table was positioned beside a worn-out recliner, a remote control resting at arm's length. A matching sofa adorned with a brown and yellow throw blanket draped over the back, faced the chair. On the opposite wall, a thirty-inch television was mounted above a cold fireplace. The mantel was cluttered with framed pictures of a boy, from infancy to adolescence. A bookcase, replete with weathered hardcover books on a diverse range of topics, displayed a wedding picture of the Schmidts.

The cornice atop the double-paned windows adorned with a sill filled with plants, gave the room a nostalgic vibe. Pierce's view of the kitchen revealed a gold-colored Formica table and two chairs on a shiny linoleum floor. Despite its modest size and sparse furnishings, the house exuded a sense of orderliness and cleanliness, down to the gray carpet that appeared to have been recently vacuumed.

To break the ice, Pierce said, "That's a nice collection of books, Mr. Schmidt."

Schmidt looked askance at the bookcase. "They belonged to my late wife. She taught linguistics at Rutgers."

"I'm sorry for your loss."

"It was a long time ago." He gestured toward the sofa. "Please, sit."

Pierce, having studied the police interview, was aware of the answer to his next question, but wanted Mr. Schmidt to feel at ease. "Did you also teach?"

"Yes. I was a science teacher."

"What field if you don't mind my asking?"

"I thought you said this would only take a few minutes?

Why are you wasting my time with these ridiculous questions?" he grumbled.

That's the end of the chitchat, thought Pierce.

"Yes, sir. I'll get right down to it, then."

He pulled out his notebook and turned a page. "You told the police that on the day Miss Robinson disappeared you were in Conneaut, Ohio visiting your twenty-two-year-old son ..." Pierce glanced at the page ... "Matthew?"

"That's right."

"Stay overnight?"

"No," he barked.

Reacting to Pierce's puzzled expression, Schmidt tempered his voice. "I turned around when I realized he wasn't home."

"Did you drive or fly to Ohio?"

"I drove."

"That's a long round-trip drive to do in one day. Didn't your son know you were coming?"

"Figured I'd surprise him."

"Why didn't you wait for him to come home?"

Schmidt ran his fingers through his thick, chestnut-colored hair and took a deep breath. "Look, my son and I aren't on the best of terms. Months go by without hearing from him. I did call when I arrived at his place, but he said he wouldn't be home for at least two days."

"Why is that?"

"I suppose his business kept him busy."

"What business is he in?"

"He runs a small business delivering books, magazines, periodicals, that sort of thing to bookstores, newsstands, and I think libraries too. When he isn't busy with that, I believe he moves small pieces of furniture if they can fit in his truck."

"You don't meet many young men living away from home and owning their own business. That's impressive."

"Is it?"

"Yes, sir."

"Yeah, well, he's very smart, like his mother."

"What's the name of his venture?"

"Is that important to your investigation?" Schmidt began tapping his foot.

"Just curious. Like I said, it's impressive for a young man to own his own business."

"Matt's Pickups & Deliveries," Schmidt answered evenly.

"Does he deliver outside of Conneaut?"

He shrugged. "Maybe."

Pierce pressed on. "If someone had a delivery out of state, let's say, in our area, would he be willing to make the trip?"

"Probably, if the pay is good, and it was a slow day."

"On that particular occasion, would he stay with you overnight?"

Schmidt stopped tapping his foot. "Are you trying to trick me?" he exclaimed. "I didn't say he's made a delivery in this area."

Hit a nerve?

"I asked because you mentioned he wouldn't be back for two days. It's possible he had an out-of-town delivery and decided to wait until the following day to return home."

Schmidt gave Pierce a wary look.

Pierce smiled, "Or he had a date and decided to spend the night elsewhere. When did he move away from home?"

"Why all this interest in my son? Schmidt demanded, his temples throbbing. "Matt wasn't even in town when that girl vanished."

"There's nothing to worry about, sir. I'm asking these types of questions of everyone who may have information that could assist me in my investigation."

He scoffed. "Knowing my son's occupation or whereabouts when that girl left won't help you find her."

Left?

"I apologize for upsetting you, but I like to be thorough to assure the parents that no stone has been left unturned."

Pierce took a second before asking his next question. "Did you happen to see or hear anything strange on the morning Miss Robinson went missing?"

"I didn't see or hear anything. I don't go around spying on the neighbors through my windows," he said, folding his arms.

"You were probably on your way to Ohio. What time did you leave for your trip?"

Schmidt's face registered confusion. He began to bounce his leg up and down. "I don't remember," he said weakly.

"Was it before the sun came up or after?"

Agitated, he stammered, "I don't ... see what that has to do ... with anything."

"Just trying to get a sense of the timeline here."

"Timeline?"

Pierce waited, observing him squirm.

Schmidt scrunched his bushy eyebrows, and said, "I think I got going around eight when I finished my breakfast."

"Thank you." Pierce wrote the time in his notepad. He flipped the page. "When the Robinsons moved in, did you welcome them to the neighborhood?"

Schmidt twitched. "I guess so. Don't remember."

"Did they ever wave hello when you were sitting on your porch or come over for a friendly chat?"

Schmidt stopped bouncing his leg. "Listen," he retorted, his voice rising, "I keep to myself. Don't like nosy neighbors coming around. And I don't think teenage girls take the time to talk to an old man like me, either. That answer your question?"

"Yes, sir."

"Hmph. Is this going to take much longer?"

"Almost done. If you don't mind me asking, what caused the rift between Matthew and you?"

Schmidt's expression shifted from furious redness to tearful sorrow. "Oh, you know how it is with fathers and sons. I wanted one thing, he wanted something else."

Pierce again referred to his notes. "You told the police you didn't get home from Ohio until close to ten p.m. That right?"

"Sounds about right."

"Did you make a stop before heading home?"

Schmidt looked everywhere but at Pierce. He faltered, "I had a sandwich, gassed up, but then I decided to have a look around town before heading home. Oh, and I also visited the Break-water Lighthouse, if that is of any significance to you," he added sarcastically.

"Never been. I've heard it's beautiful."

"It's nice."

"How long ago did your son move to Ohio?"

"After graduating high school in 2005, he moved to Columbus to attend Ohio State."

"Oh, Yeah? What did he major in?"

Schmidt let out a tired breath. "Science. After his degree, he didn't pursue a Ph.D as required for research, so he gave up job hunting in his field and started his own business. Any other questions about my son?" he glared.

Ignoring the attitude, Pierce inquired casually, "How did he end up in Conneaut?"

"Picked it out of a hat I think. That boy's adventurous."

"Does he come home on holidays, or for the summer?"

"Uh … he visits when he can."

"When was the last time he came home?"

Schmidt rubbed his prickly chin. "I don't know. Maybe August or September?"

Pierce closed his notepad and stood. "Thank you for your time."

Before leaving, he pointed to the framed pictures on the mantel.

"Matthew?"

Schmidt sadly stared at the pictures. "Yes, that's Matt."

"Handsome boy."

Schmidt nodded.

"Goodbye, sir," Pierce said, resolute in delving deeper into Matthew Schmidt's life.

Josef Schmidt closed and bolted the front door. He then proceeded to the window and cautiously peeked through the curtains. He remained there until Pierce had driven away and then picked up the telephone.

---

22

*P*ierce returned to the office ready to piece together the information he'd acquired that day. After his conversation with Josef Schmidt, he wanted to ascertain whether a relationship existed between the Schmidt and Robinson families before deciding on his next steps.

Despite his aversion to Mrs. Robinson thinking he had news when she heard his voice, he had no choice, and dialed.

"Mrs. Robinson. This is Howard Pierce."

"Yes, Mr. Pierce. Have you any news?" she asked expectantly.

"No ma'am. It's still early in my investigation. The reason I'm calling is that during my visit, I forgot to ask if your husband and you are friendly with your neighbors?"

"I don't understand. Do you think one of our neighbors might know where my daughter is?" she asked, her voice trembling.

Damn!

"Oh no, ma'am," Pierce said hastily. "I'm merely trying to get a feel for the people who reside in your neighborhood."

"A feel?"

"It's a small community, and I'm curious to know if everybody gets along and there are no issues."

"Yes, everyone gets along here," she responded with a hint of impatience.

Careful not to give her a reason to suspect the Schmidts, Pierce inquired, "Was Maceen in school with any of the neighborhood teens?"

"What? No, the kids around here are younger than my daughter, and I believe Mr. Schmidt's son is older than Maceen and doesn't live here anymore."

"He away at college?"

"I think so," she sighed. "The last time I saw that young man, it was either late August or early September, but I'm not certain. The Schmidts aren't particularly friendly."

"Thank you for your time, Mrs. Robinson. I'm sorry to have disturbed you."

"Goodbye," she said curtly, and hung up.

Years of experience interviewing suspects had sharpened Pierce's intuition. Josef Schmidt was hiding something, perhaps a connection between his son, Matthew, and Maceen. Not wanting to waste another minute, he decided to trust his gut.

As Matthew Schmidt had not undergone a background check, Pierce did the verification. No criminal record was discovered. Pierce then conducted a search for Matt's Pickups & Deliveries in Conneaut, Ohio. Despite the absence of a physical storefront, he found an obsolete website, which had not been updated for several months, and did not have a telephone number or an email associated with the business.

He hit pay dirt when a search for Schmidt, an uncommon name in the small town of less than 13,000 inhabitants, listed the same hidden telephone number as the one he discovered in Maceen's bedroom.

Another piece of the puzzle.

He repeatedly tapped his pen on his desk, contemplating

whether dialing the number would alert someone receiving a call with the East Stroudsburg, 570 area code. He took the chance and dialed it. A recorded message of a man's voice responded, "Please leave your name and number and a brief message and I will get back to you."

Pierce hung up without leaving a message. He then turned his attention to the computer.

At first look, Schmidt did not appear to have a Facebook account or any other social media presence. Fortunately, Pierce stumbled upon an old MySpace account. A photo of an acne-ridden, shaggy-haired, Matthew Schmidt, wearing a black v-neck t-shirt and a cocky smile, was featured on the site. He sent the page to the printer.

Pierce wondered if he could find a more recent photograph of Matthew Schmidt in an archived yearbook. After searching the Ohio State University's website and failing to find the information, he resorted to the internet and found the 2009 yearbook, the year Schmidt received his Bachelor of Science degree in biology with a focus on plant science. *The pieces are coming together.*

Not only did it include his graduation picture, but one other of him posing with his science lab classmates. Matthew wore his hair closely shaved on the sides and long on top. His piercing gaze locked onto the camera, and his radiant smile lit up his face.

Pierce printed the photos.

Using his private detective credentials, Pierce was given access to the Department of Motor Vehicles in Cleveland. That search provided him with Matthew Schmidts' home address and his vehicle registration information.

He sent the pages to the printer and logged off the computer.

Collecting the printouts, he placed them in a separate folder from the one Detective Leung had given him, and marked it 'Schmidt.'

Satisfied, Pierce sat back, closed his eyes and considered his options. He could send Frank to Conneaut, envisioning the various scenarios that could unfold if Frank were successful in finding Maceen. Ultimately, Pierce recognized that he had to go himself.

To avoid a five-hour drive to Conneaut, Pierce booked a one-way ticket to Cleveland International Airport. There, he'll pick up a rental car and drive the rest of the way into town.

23

$\mathcal{T}$he front door abruptly flung open. Images of her abusive ex-husband thrust Ruby into survival mode. Her hand reached for the drawer where she kept the revolver— the one she had never fired outside the shooting range.

In burst Frank.

"Damn, Frank," screamed Ruby, heart thumping. "What the fuck? I almost shot you."

Frank gasped, "Sorry ... Ruby ... I have news."

"What news got you running in here scaring me half to death?" asked Ruby, slamming her desk drawer close.

He shot her a goofy grin, and approached her. "I think I know what happened to that girl."

"You mean, Maceen Robinson?"

"The very one, Ruby."

Ruby raised an eyebrow, her moment of fright receding. "So you've cracked the case, have you?"

"You bet." He pointed his chin toward Pierce's office door. "Howard in?"

"He's in but doesn't want to be disturbed."

Frank dropped into the seat next to her desk. "Any idea when he'll be free?"

"You know better than to ask."

Frank clicked his tongue. "Yeah." He slumped into the seat.

"Well? Are you going to tell me, or do I have to hear it from the boss?"

Frank pushed his chair closer. "I wanted the boss to hear it first, but I guess I can fill you in."

"I'm all ears, Frank. Lay it on me."

Meanwhile, as Pierce sifted through the papers on his desk, he contemplated the possibility of finding Maceen alive and well. if so, would she be willing to come home? Or, if he were to fail to locate her, how long would he be willing to remain in Conneaut chasing a hunch?

As he pondered these questions, he heard a commotion outside his office. He waited for Ruby to rush in and explain the disturbance. When she didn't show, he shrugged and began a search for a car rental company at Cleveland airport.

As he stepped out of the office, he walked over to the printer to retrieve his paperwork. Frank and Ruby were engrossed in a private conversation, oblivious to his presence as the constant hum of the printer filled the air.

What are they up to? he thought, grabbing the papers from the printer.

"What's going on?" Pierce asked.

They abruptly ended their conversation. Frank sprung off the chair and announced, "I have news."

"Okay. Take a deep breath and tell me all about your news in my office."

Ruby gave Frank a thumbs up. He winked in return.

Frank began yammering before Pierce sat in his chair. "At first I thought Oliver had something to do with Maceen's disappearance. That boy's in love with her, and he sure as hell is hiding something. But he's too unsure of himself to have declared his love to Maceen. No, it's like I've been saying all along. I believe Maceen Robinson met a guy and fell head over heels. He convinced her to elope with him, and while we don't know where they are, I'm pretty sure that's the reason she left home. Both Oliver and Cindy confirmed that Maceen told them she had met a guy." He grinned from ear to ear.

"Does this guy have a name?"

Frank beamed. "Yes."

"Well?"

"I managed to get his name outta Oliver, but it was like pulling teeth!" Frank chuckled, his voice filled with excitement. "His name is Matt," he exclaimed, as if he had discovered a hidden treasure.

Pierce decided to have a little fun with his overly enthusiastic assistant. "This morning I met with a Josef Schmidt who has a son named Matthew," commented Pierce matter-of-factly.

"You don't suppose it's ..." Frank started to say, but stopped when he realized Pierce was toying with him.

"Wait. It's the same Matt, right?"

"Yes."

"Matthew Schmidt" Frank said, laughing.

"According to the police report, Mr. Schmidt asserted he was out of town the day Maceen left home, but after meeting with him, I got the impression he was not totally forthcoming."

Frank nodded.

Pierce shuffled the papers on his desk and retrieved a photo. He pushed it toward Frank. "This is Matthew Schmidt."

Frank studied it. "Nice looking guy."

"Tell you what, keep the photo and run over to the library." He looked at his watch. "If you hurry, you might be able to catch Oliver to see if he can identify it."

"Oliver said Maceen never showed up to the library with her new boyfriend."

"Perhaps he visited the library another time, and Oliver

might have met him then. Or if Oliver is hiding something, as you suggested, he may have met Matthew at another time."

"The thing is, Oliver drove off when we finished our conversation."

"All right. I believe we have sufficient information to identify Matthew Schmidt as our primary suspect. Here's where we are: Matthew Schmidt runs a small business delivering periodicals and other items within his local area. His father mentioned that he hadn't seen his son since last summer. Mrs. Robinson said that she might have seen Matthew last August or September. It's plausible Matt and Maceen connected then. He may have come into town a few weeks prior to Maceen's clandestine departure, they crossed paths, and got to talking. During their interaction, he captivated her interest in botany and presented her with a cranberry plant."

"Cranberry?"

"Yes. His yearbook page says Matthew holds a bachelor's degree in biology with a focus on plant science. Perhaps he convinced her to rendezvous with him early that October morning, I'm thinking to visit the Tannersville Cranberry Bog."

"Because of her sudden interest in botany?"

"Exactly. Also, Maceen did not take any belongings with her other than what she was wearing. If she were fleeing, she would have taken clothes, toiletries, and other essentials. I firmly believe Maceen had every intention of returning home that day. Everything points to a carefully executed plan."

"Or Matt is her prince and she decided to run away with him."

"As I've said before, we can't jump to conclusions. We still lack all the necessary information to form a complete picture, but as of now, I agree that all avenues lead to that possibility." Frank's gathering of information from Cindy and Oliver, coupled with Maceen's former manager's insights, and the interviews conducted with her parents and Josef Schmidt, further solidified Pierce's belief that they were on the right track.

Tomorrow morning I'm flying to Cleveland to hopefully fill in the missing pieces."

"Oh?"

"I'm determined to learn what happened on the morning of October 24th."

"So you think there's a chance she's still alive?"

Pierce sighed. "I hope so, Frank."

"How long do you think you'll be gone?"

"I hope I won't be spending more than a day there, but if I need to, I'll find a motel."

"Stay safe. You don't know what kind of man this Matthew is."

"It's as you said, he may turn out to be a prince. If not, I'm sure I can deal with him. My priority is finding Maceen alive."

"Yeah. Good luck, boss. I hope you find her."

24

Wednesday, March 24, 2010

*U*pon his arrived at Cleveland International Airport at 9:40 a.m., Pierce promptly called Louise to assure her he had arrived safely. After securing his rental car, he tossed his carry-on bag onto the front passenger seat, programmed the GPS for Conneaut, and fidgeted with the radio dial until he found a local oldies station he could tolerate. He was all set for the 83-mile drive.

Pierce, having eaten a small coffee cake with a cup of coffee while waiting to board his plane, arrived in Cleveland famished but eager to get to Conneaut, he decided to find a place to eat there.

In downtown Conneaut, he cruised through the town. A diner caught his eye, and he promptly pulled into the parking lot.

Waiting to be seated, Pierce soaked in the room's atmosphere buzzing with lively conversations of the latest news, the weather, gas prices, and the Cleveland Indians. One of three waitresses, dressed in the restaurant's signature pastel green uniform featuring a white collar, short sleeves, and an apron, greeted him warmly as she picked up a steaming pot of coffee. "Come on in," she said, her mascara and blue eyeliner glistening, as she pointed to the seats at the counter. "Have a seat. I'll be with you in a minute." She dashed off to top off the coffee for the customer beckoning her for a refill.

Only two stools remained unoccupied. Pierce took the one farthest from the door, a habit from his days as a homicide detective. A customer across from him exchanged a friendly nod with Pierce.

"Coffee?" asked the waitress approaching him with a well-practiced smile as she picked up his coffee cup.

"Yes, please."

She poured from the carafe, and grabbed a menu. "Breakfast is over, but if you want eggs, I'm sure we can accommodate you."

"Thank you."

"My name's Darlene. Let me know when you're ready to order," she said, disappearing through the kitchen doors.

Pierce savored the strong coffee, while examining the menu. Darlene emerged from the kitchen, her forearms laden with plates. He observed her deftly placing them in front of hungry diners. That done, she turned to Pierce with pencil and pad in hand. "Ready?"

"Yes. I'd like a grilled cheese on white with tomato, and a cup of chicken noodle soup."

"You got it." She scribbled his order in her pad, and sauntered off to the kitchen.

Pierce glanced around. "Is it always this busy?" he asked the man sitting beside him.

"Most folks here take their lunch break at the same time. It'll be a bit quieter soon. Visiting?" he asked.

"Yes. My nephew."

"I hope you enjoy our little town."

"Thank you."

He wiped his mouth and snatched the check lying on the counter. On his way to the cashier, he said, "Try the apple pie before you leave. Best in town."

"Maybe I will. Thanks."

Darlene emerged from the kitchen a few minutes later carrying his order.

Although Pierce had obtained an address for Matthew Schmidt from his background check, Schmidt might have moved to a different location. "Darlene, do you know where I might find Matt's Pickups & Deliveries?" he asked as she placed his lunch in front of him.

"Oh, they don't have a physical store. You'll have to call them to set up an appointment."

"Do you happen to have their telephone number?"

"I've never used their services, but I'm sure you can find them in the phone book."

"I tried that, but that number is not in service."

"That's odd. I'm sure I've seen their truck in the area, but maybe they've gone out of business." Darlene tapped her pencil on her pad, contemplating for a moment. "If you need something delivered, I know someone who might be able to help you."

"That's kind of you, Darlene. But I need to find the owner on a personal matter."

At the far end of the counter sat a weathered man, his wrinkled red shirt, overalls, and unkempt hair and beard revealing a dire need for a haircut and shave. He fixed his intense gaze on Pierce. "Are you a policeman?" he bellowed, causing a simultaneous turning of heads.

Aware of the elderly man and his apparent interest in him since he entered the restaurant, Pierce responded, "No, sir."

"If you don't need a delivery and you're not a policeman, why are you so interested in Matt's whatchamacallit?"

"Respectfully, sir. That's my business."

He scoffed, and snapped, "Margo give me my check, will ya?"

Smiling, the waitress who had attended him, ripped the ticket from her pad and set it in front of him. "Here you go. Have a pleasant day, Pete."

He picked up the check and mumbled incoherently as he made his way to the cashier.

Darlene remarked, "That's Pete. Don't worry about him; he's the town gossip. Lost his wife a few years back, and now he busies himself with other people's business."

Nosy people can be useful, thought Pierce.

"He lives close by. Comes in here everyday for breakfast and lunch. His wife did all the cooking, but now that she's gone, he eats some of his meals here. It's all so sad."

"Lots of lonely people in this world, Darlene."

"Sure are," she replied. "Better eat your lunch before it gets cold," she advised, then turned her attention to the customer calling for his check.

After finishing his meal, Pierce bought a large coffee to go, and after a moment of indecision, a slice of apple pie. Before leaving, he caught Darlene's attention, and made sure to give her a generous tip.

As Pierce walked toward the rental, he noticed Pete seated in his rusty pickup truck. He clicked the key fob and carefully put his package next to his carry-on before proceeding to the pickup.

"Hey, pal," he greeted, startling Pete who was busy going through the local paper he had plucked out of the trash on his way out of the diner. "Mind if I ask you a couple of questions?"

Pete smirked. "I knew you were a cop."

"I'm not a cop, but I'd like to know your concern with my asking about Matthew's Pickups and Deliveries."

Pete scratched his bristly beard, his voice weak. "No reason."

"Do you know Matthew Schmidt?"

Pete looked away, a hint of embarrassment in his eyes. "Everyone around here knows Schmidt," he mumbled.

"Oh yeah? Know where he lives?"

"Nope. Never been invited."

"How about his phone number? Know that?"

Pete again scratched his beard. "Ain't ever had a reason to call him."

"Okay," Pierce smiled. "Have a nice day."

Despite Pete's suspicious behavior, Pierce did not believe he knew much about Matthew Schmidt. He set the GPS and proceeded to Schmidt's last known address.

When he arrived, Pierce circled the block and parked two blocks away. On his leisurely walk around the neighborhood, he admired the three and four-story apartment buildings on the tree-lined streets. They appeared to have been constructed decades ago. There was no garbage on the sidewalks or garbage cans without their lids securely on. Some stoops were adorned with heavy cement planters filled with plants beginning to bud.

Nice.

A woman pushing a baby stroller came walking up the street. When she got close, Pierce nodded. She gave him a careful smile, then picked up her pace.

At the assumed address, Pierce promptly rang the doorbell for apartment three, but no one answered.

Returning to his car, Pierce decided to park it closer to Matt's building so he could keep vigil. After an hour, people began arriving home, filling up the last empty parking spaces. Pierce peeked at his watch—five thirty. He popped the lid of his coffee container, took a swig of the tepid coffee, and put it in the cup holder. Reaching for the takeout bag, he pulled out the container and fork, and began devouring the pie between gulps of coffee. *That guy wasn't lying. Excellent pie.*

After a while, Pierce felt the urgent need to relieve himself.

With no one coming or going from the apartment, he decided to find a nearby gas station, risking the loss of his parking space.

GPS directed him one mile away where he pulled in, stretched his legs and used the facilities. He splashed cold water on his face to shake off drowsiness. At the counter, he bought a large container of coffee. *Louise will kill me if she finds out how much coffee I've had today.*

Afraid he'd doze off waiting for Schmidt to come home, he decided to cruise around town, hoping to spot Matt's vehicle. Not five minutes on the road, a red truck sped by, matching the description of Matt's truck that he retrieved from the DMV. Instinctively, Pierce followed.

When the driver stopped at a factory to pick up boxes, Pierce identified Matthew Schmidt. For the next hour and a half, Matt hopped in and out of the truck, picking up and delivering merchandise to various locations. Pierce remained in the background, finishing his coffee and patiently awaiting Schmidt's seemingly endless workday.

Matt finally arrived in his neighborhood and circled the block twice until he spotted someone pull out of the same spot Pierce had abandoned to find a gas station.

What luck! thought Pierce as he drove past. It took him fifteen minutes of circling around the neighborhood to find parking four blocks away.

After touching base with Louise and texting Frank an update, he turned off the radio and walked to apartment three.

This is it.

Adrenaline coursed through his body as he rang the doorbell. *If my instincts are correct, Maceen will be there. If I'm wrong, I'll have to go back to square one.*

When the door opened, Pierce experienced a profound sense of relief.

"Hello Maceen."

EPILOGUE

*M*aceen's story began the day she first laid eyes on Matthew Schmidt. On that fateful morning, as she hurried to her car, her cap flew off. Determined to retrieve it before it landed in the empty lot next door, she gave chase. Finally, she managed to snag it and looked around, hoping no one had witnessed her wild pursuit. That's when she noticed him—seated on his father's porch, puffing on a cigarette and watching her. His shining smile sent a blush across her cheeks.

Days later, as Maceen was leaving the mall after work, she unexpectedly ran into him. She was about to walk to her car when she heard a voice call out, "Hey!"

Turning her head, she saw Matt saunter over with his cheerful smile and sparkling eyes. "Hello," he greeted her.

"Hi," she responded, her voice barely above a whisper. "What are you doing here?" she asked, feeling a bit self-conscious, noticing the shopping bag in his hand.

"Doing a little shopping." And you?"

"I work here," Maceen said.

"Oh, yeah? Where?"

"Bon-tons. I'm just getting off work."

"My name's Matt, by the way. And yours?"

"Maceen. Are you related to Mr. Schmidt?"

"I'm his son."

"Oh, I didn't know he had a son," she said, feeling foolish for saying that.

He smiled. "I've been living in Ohio and rarely come up to visit. Can I buy you a burger or something?"

Maceen was taken aback by his sudden offer. She typically declined invitations from strangers, but something about him compelled her to accept.

Thus began a relationship that gradually led to Maceen's distraction, secrecy, and deception—a transformative relationship that profoundly changed her life.

She was aware that her parents would disapprove of her relationship with Matt. Even her best friend, Cindy, would object to their age gap. However, he was unlike the immature boys in her school, who always had a witty remark ready when she passed them by. She yearned to spend every waking moment in Matt's company. But it wasn't easy—Something had to give. Maceen cut her study time at the library with Oliver, missed an occasional after-school hike, and ultimately quit her weekend job.

To avoid bumping into anyone she knew, they sometimes met in the town of Wilson, approximately thirty miles away. There, they would catch a movie or grab a bite. Sometimes, they'd rendezvous in other towns away from home. Those stolen moments together were like a dream come true for Maceen. She could spend hours listening to him.

Maceen was particularly impressed with Matt's extensive knowledge of botany, a subject she never dreamed she'd be interested in. She attentively listened to him ramble on about the process of plant cultivation, particularly the cultivation of challenging varieties that thrive in bog environments. When he suggested she buy a book on botany, she chose one specifically about bog plants, which was the last topic they had discussed.

She diligently read it from cover to cover within a single night, proudly expressing her love for the book, though secretly comprehending only a fraction of its content. A week after purchasing it, Matt surprised her with a gift.

They had arranged to meet at the back of the mall's parking lot, where Sears is located. As she approached his vehicle, she nervously checked her surroundings, fearing that someone, possibly a neighbor or one of her friends, would see her. When Matt saw her, he got out of his vehicle and picked up a box from his front passenger seat. "Hold out your hands," he instructed her, when she got closer.

With anticipation, she complied as he said. He carefully placed the box in her hands. Inside, she gazed at an oblong planter filled with soil. Feeling a bit clever, she asked, "What kind of seeds do I plant in here?"

Matt chuckled. "None, Maceen. I've already planted cranberry seeds in there for you."

"Oh?" She raised an eyebrow.

"Yes, as you probably remember from the last time we spoke, cranberries are hard to cultivate at home," he explained.

"Sure," remarked Maceen, not at all sure.

"Don't worry. I've already stratified the seeds. Do you remember what that means?"

Maceen paused for a moment, trying to recall the key points of stratification. With a broad smile, she proudly announced, "I know! You soak the seeds in water for one to three days, then mix them with soil and place them in the refrigerator ... uh ... for about three months?"

"Very good, Maceen. Now, all you need to do is put the planter on a sunny windowsill, make sure to keep the soil moist, and wait for the shoots to sprout."

"Thank you again," she said, vowing she'd take care of it.

"One more thing," he added. "I wrote my business number on the bottom of the planter, in case you want to talk. I may not answer right away, but leave a message and I'll call you back."

As much as she would have liked, late-night phone calls with him wouldn't be happening. His out-of-state number appearing on her parent's phone bill, would raise questions she was not prepared to answer. "I will," she replied. "Thank you."

"You're welcome."

He took the box from her. "I'll put it in the car for you."

They walked the few steps to her car, where he carefully put the box on the front passenger seat, and secured it with the seatbelt.

Maceen smiled at his thoughtfulness.

He closed her car door, and said, "I have an idea. How about we plan a trip to the Tannersville Cranberry Bog? While there, I can show you how to identify the diverse flora and fauna in the area."

"Yes, I'd love that." Maceen said enthusiastically.

"We'll have to sneak in before dawn to avoid bumping into the crowds," he casually said.

That gave her pause. "But how will we be able to see anything?"

"Don't worry. I know my way around the bog, and I'll have my big flashlight with me. It'll be fine. I know a way to sneak in. I've done it lots of times. So, are you game?"

Maceen wasn't thrilled about sneaking in and was nervous about the early hour. She wondered how she was going to tell her parents about leaving the house so early.

She didn't want to let him down. His enthusiasm made her think he knew what he was doing. Despite her reservations, she forced a smile and replied, "Sure, I'm in."

For the next few days, Maceen couldn't focus on her schoolwork, preoccupied with the consequences of her parents' dismay if they discovered her plans. She also had to figure out how to leave home, and upon her return, explain her actions to her parents and friends, whom she would also have to deceive. After a sleepless night, she thought she had it all figured out.

—

Saturday, October 24, 2009

MACEEN WAS a mixture of excitement and nervousness when they arrived in Tannersville. She almost told Matt she didn't want to sneak into the cranberry bog, but was afraid of appearing cowardly. Matt took her by the hand as they carefully navigated the murky marshland of rocky outcrops and dense foliage, illuminated by the flickering glow of his flashlight. The occasional animal sounds unnerved Maceen. Matt sensed her discomfort and tried to distract her. As they proceeded further into the bog, he kept pointing his flashlight at the vegetation, explaining its name and how it contributed to the bog. Maceen barely paid attention. Her focus remained fixed on her surroundings, fearful that an unseen bear or bobcat could strike at any moment.

Stepping onto the floating boardwalk, Maceen struggled to maintain her balance as the bog water spilled onto the plank with her every step. From the corner of her eye, she caught a fleeting glimpse of something scatter away. "What was that?" she asked, her voice trembling with nervousness.

"It's merely an otter," Matt assured her. "They're harmless."

As soon as he uttered those words, the piercing screech of an owl startled Maceen, causing her to lose her footing. She stumbled, causing the walkway to lean to one side, splashing water all over her. Matt swiftly pulled her to her feet and enveloped her in his arms. As he held her, Maceen let out her fears and guilt in a torrent of tears.

"It's all right, Maceen. It's just an owl. It won't hurt you." He stroked her hair.

When she calmed, Matt kissed her forehead, and slowly worked his way to her eyes and cheeks until he found her mouth. Maceen pulled back and stared into his eyes, but he drew her closer and kissed her again. Of course, they had kissed before, but, perhaps due to her intense emotional state, her senses were heightened. She had never experienced such a profound longing, and hungrily surrendered to his kisses, forgetting her guilt and no longer afraid of the world around her.

"Hey, let's not rush this," Matt whispered, his voice filled with emotion, and gently broke free from their embrace. "Let's get out of here." He grabbed her hand and led her out of the bog, both lost in their own thoughts.

Back in the truck, he reached for her. They spent an hour on the back seat of his vehicle, wrapped in each other's arms, as the sun peaked over the horizon and the day warmed. While Maceen had cherished their intimacy, when it was over, she felt ashamed and quickly got dressed, unable to meet his gaze.

Matt opened the car door and walked around to her side. He extended his hand for her to step out. "Maceen," he asked, "are you okay?" Overwhelmed with emotion, she began to weep. Mortified for what she had done, she couldn't imagine facing her parents.

Matt gently guided her to the front seat and reached into the glove compartment and pulled out a napkin to dry her eyes. She wiped away her tears and blew her nose, muttering, "I can't go home." She deposited the napkin into a small trash container in the truck's cup holder.

Matt hung his head unsure of what to do. When he looked at her, he asked, "Would you like to crash at my place until you're ready to go home?"

Maceen realized that Matt lived far away, and that the longer she stayed away from home, the harder it would be for her to return. However, the profound sense of guilt she felt, not only for deceiving her parents, but more significantly, for succumbing to her passion, prevented her from telling him to take her home.

"Yes," she breathed, a hint of relief in her voice. She was temporarily avoiding confronting her parents until she could concoct a plausible excuse or muster the courage to tell them the truth.

More than an hour passed since they left Tannersville—Maceen, gazing out the car window at the passing traffic, while Matt focused on driving, dreading saying the wrong thing and further upsetting her.

"How much longer?" Maceen suddenly asked, without turning her head away from the window.

"We're not even halfway there. It'll be a while," Matt replied, relieved she had finally spoken.

"I didn't realize you lived so far away," she whispered as if to herself. "I mean, I know you live in Ohio, but do you think ...

"Maceen, if you want to go home, I'll turn this car around."

She turned to him. "It's just" ...

"What?"

"My parents are going to freak," she said in a shaky voice.

"Why don't you call them?"

"Are you crazy?" she shrieked. "What could I possibly say? That I snuck out of the house to meet someone they don't know to traipse around the cranberry bog in the dark? How do you think they'd react?" She teared up again.

"It's all right, Maceen. I'll do whatever you want me to do."

"Let's just keep going," she said. "I'll figure it out." Once more, she turned her head toward the car window, watching the miles roll by. These miles would carry her away from all that was familiar to her. Her mind was filled with fleeting images of the passionate romance she was currently experiencing and her parents' distress wondering where she was.

Maceen's reverie was interrupted when Matt parked at a rest stop.

"Feeling better?" he asked.

"Yes.," she lied. Can we get something to eat?"

"Of course. After I fill up, we can go inside, have something to eat, and get some water, and whatever else you'd like."

In the restroom, Maceen decided to stop crying and accept the consequences of her actions. She took a deep breath, washed her face, and with a determined spirit to make the most of her situation, prepared to face Matt. He flagged her over to a table where he was waiting with a couple of burgers, fries, and cold beverages. She devoured the meal as if she hadn't eaten in days.

When they were done eating, Matt asked, "Are you sure you don't want me to take you back home?"

"I'm sure. Let's keep going."

When she turned on her cellphone, the sound of the first expected phone call from home abruptly shattered her resolve. She stared at her phone until the message icon popped up. After several minutes, Maceen listened to her mom's anxious voice. "Maceen, where are you? Are you all right? Please call me," her mother pleaded. She had been calling since discovering Maceen's note. She rang her every hour after that, her voice becoming increasingly frantic with each message she left. By the time her father called that evening, Maceen couldn't bear to listen to the desperation in their voices and turned off her phone. After a while, she asked Matt to listen to the messages, but once again, she refused his offer to take her back home.

The next day, Cindy started calling and texting Maceen daily. With each communication, Maceen's anxiety grew until Matt suggested she turn off her phone permanently.

Maceen didn't dare venture out of Matt's apartment, fearing someone may recognize her. She was tempted to call Oliver, who knew her secret, but she reasoned that by now, he had shared it with everyone, especially the police. She regretted trusting him, and each day, she feared the possibility of the police knocking on the door.

Matt reassured her that most people in their community hadn't even heard about her disappearance, and if they had, they wouldn't remember her appearance the next day. Despite Matt's reassurances, Maceen was terrified and remained holed up in the apartment for weeks.

Weeks turned into months, and Maceen felt increasingly disconnected from her past life. She knew people were searching for her, and that her parents were heartbroken, but despite her sympathy for them, her shame held her back from reaching out. She was battling an inner conflict between her new life and her desire to return home to her family.

In the end, she decided to settle down with the man she had grown to love more each day. Eventually, she got a job working at a nursery where she discovered a passion for plant care and flourished in her new role.

Christmas was hard. Maceen longed to be home with her family. Matt did everything he could to cheer her up by decorating the apartment, taking her out to see the town's decorations, and treating her to a Christmas dinner that reminded her of home. On Christmas morning, he presented her with an engagement ring. A month before her eighteenth birthday, she sent away for her birth certificate. A week later, they were married in a city hall ceremony.

When Matt's father called to warn him that a private detective was snooping around and asking questions about him, he failed to inform Maceen. He was concerned that the detective would likely catch up to them sooner or later, but despite this worry, Matt relaxed, happy that he and Maceen were married and that no one, not even a private detective, could force his wife to return home to Pennsylvania.

However, when Pierce showed up at their door, Maceen was relieved she'd been found.

AUTHOR'S NOTE

My best friend in high school, Maribel, inspired the story of *Where's Maceen?* Maribel was a pretty and talented girl with an opera-worthy soprano voice. In junior high, our music teacher cast her as the lead role in *Aida*, and she did an amazing job.

I spent almost every day with Maribel and her younger sister, Iris. Her mom once joked that I was visiting them so often that she could see my face in her soup. To say we were close is an understatement.

One day, Iris summoned me to my third-floor apartment window with her usual high-pitched whistle that would make most boys jealous. When I got there, Maribel wasn't with her. Iris was worried and asked me to come down.

I didn't feel like hanging out with them that day, but seeing her face, I knew something had happened.

"Maribel ran away from home, and we don't know where she

is," she blurted as soon as I got there. "Antonio has been all over the neighborhood looking for her, but no one has seen her."

If their brother, Antonio, couldn't find her, I thought. Something bad must have happened to her. He knew everyone in the neighborhood.

For the next few weeks, Maribel's family lived in a nightmare. There was no mention of getting the police involved. Her single mother had lost faith in the police after Antonio got stabbed in the neighborhood, and no one was arrested.

But this story has a happy ending. Maribel finally returned home and told her mom and siblings where she had been and why she couldn't come home right away. She had fallen in love with a much older man she had been secretly seeing. Once she lost her virginity to him, Maribel felt she could not face her mother.

When we finally talked, all she could do was blubber about how happy she was. I was hurt she had not confided in me and secretly upset by her confession. In the end, she married him and they had a child. But a few years later, he left her for a much younger girl.

It is estimated that approximately 1.6 to 2.8 million individuals in the United States are considered runaways or throwaway children, primarily due to circumstances such as parental abandonment, family conflicts, physical or emotional abuse, or neglect. The numbers below are resources if you should ever need them.

NCMEC - National Center for Missing and Exploited Children
(24 hours) 1-800-843-5678

Youth & Teens in Crisis - The National Runaway Safeline
1-800-Runaway

National Runaway Safeline
1-800-786-2929

ACKNOWLEDGMENTS

Hey, my consulting team! Mary Anne Moore, Kelly Jensen, Susan Moore Jordan, Sahar Abdulaziz, and Belinda Gordon (who has done an amazing job formatting my books)—I appreciate your valuable feedback and unwavering support. It helped me get to the finish line. Gracias y Amor, mi amigas!

Wesley Goulartt—My deepest gratitude for your incredible talent as a cover designer. Thank you for your patience and perseverance in dealing with all the changes. It's always a pleasure working with you.

To my family and friends, I realize that life can get hectic, and I totally get it if you're not into mystery books or reading novels in general. But let me tell you, your encouragement means the world to me.

Last, but definitely not least, I want to thank you, husband of mine. Throughout all my ramblings about my novel, you've been my unwavering support system. You're all right, Amor mio.

ABOUT THE AUTHOR

Mystery writer, Evelyn Infante, had an interesting idea: she wanted to create a homicide detective. It was a fun challenge for her, yet she didn't want to copy the weird or emotional detectives she saw in movies and TV shows. Instead, she created a detective who is happily married, loyal, smart, and always pays attention. That's what makes a great detective, right?

Evelyn is the author of Simply Gregg and Bloodhound Investigations, which earned her a Fofky's Readers' Choice Award for Best Eclectic Book. *Where's Maceen?* is the third installment in the 'Howard Pierce Investigates' series.

But her literary journey in the mystery genre is far from over. She is actively working on her next novel. A tantalizing hint—it will prominently feature Frank Irizarry, Howard Pierce's assistant.

ALSO BY EVELYN INFANTE

SIMPLY GREGG

BLOODHOUND INVESTIGATIONS

FIND EVELYN ON THE WEB

https://shaggy-dog-books.com/evelyn-infante/
facebook.com/@writing4joy
instagram.com/evelyninfante99
linkedin.com/evelyn infante author

www.ingramcontent.com/pod-product-compliance
Lightning Source LLC
Chambersburg PA
CBHW051245170626
46809CB00004B/1493